TRUSTING HIM

ITALIAN LOVERS (BOOK 3)

DIANA FRASER

BAY BOOKS

Trusting Him
(Also published as The Passionate Italian)
by Diana Fraser

© 2011 Diana Fraser

—Italian Romance Series—

The Italian's Perfect Lover
Seduced by the Italian
The Passionate Italian
An Accidental Christmas

For more information about Diana and to sign up to her newsletter, visit www.dianafraser.com.

CHAPTER 1

hat the hell was going on?

Rose stared at the email once more in disbelief.

It seemed her sleeping business partner had woken up and sold their company—hers, in all but name. But it was the last sentence that had her really worried.

He'd also sold her services for six months as part of the deal.

Stunned, she pushed the laptop away and stared, unseeing, at the waves breaking onto the beach to the rear of her cottage.

How could she have been so stupid? She should have paid her partner off by now but she'd thought having someone else's name on the paperwork made her untraceable.

Ha! That was a joke.

She grabbed a wrap that lay over the back of her ancient couch and flung open the rickety French windows that led directly to the beach. Her wild, curly hair lifted and whirled in the fresh wind as she scrunched through heavy sand towards the shore. She scanned the horizon but failed to find the sense of peace the beautiful, white-flecked bay usually gave her.

Here in New Zealand, half a world away from her old life, she'd felt hidden, unfindable. But someone had just bought her company for much more than it was worth. This wasn't business; this was personal.

She turned to look at the lone cottage, nestled in the native bush between cliff and sea that had been her world—her business and her home—for the past two years, but no more.

She would have to leave.

There could only be one person persistent enough and with enough reason to seek her out. There was only one person who wanted her enough.

Giovanni Visconti—her husband.

She closed her eyes and tried to block out the memories, concentrating on the sting of the sand as it hit her bare legs, on the clatter of the New Zealand flax, alive in the fresh northerly and on the damp of the fine mist that rose from the pounding waves.

A shiver coursed through her body that had nothing to do with the chill breeze and everything to do with her husband.

Giovanni. Just the feel of his name upon her lips recalled the heat of his mouth upon hers and memories she needed to forget.

She crouched down, head in hands, and tried to control the panic that threatened to overwhelm her.

There had been many reasons to leave him—his jealousy for one, her need for independence for another—but it had been neither of these things. Giovanni had never known the catalyst for her leaving. And, if she had her way, he never would. Her secret could destroy him. And she couldn't do that to the man she loved.

She jumped up and looked at her watch. She didn't have

much time. She had to move on. She couldn't risk seeing him because she didn't know if she'd have the strength to leave him again.

She entered the rear of the cottage and scanned the room, mentally calculating what she'd need to take with her. Not much. She'd come with nothing. She could start again with nothing.

Computer of course; the few photos of her family that her mother had managed to retain; and—

Her eyes rested on the front door, just visible in the shadows on the far side of the open-plan cottage. It was open.

She froze. She'd left it closed. It was always closed. Her life was private. She always used the back door.

She held her breath, listening intently, but all she could hear and see were the flapping of papers pinned to her wall, pages turning on an open book on her table and the fine silk of the curtains curling and snapping back in the constant breeze. But still she felt a clammy chill crawl up her spine before settling at her neck.

Someone was here.

She turned to close the French windows, cursing under her breath as the old wooden doors, swollen with sea air, squeaked stiffly together before banging shut.

"Ah, my English Rose, still with the common touch." His voice was ice-cold.

She closed her eyes as shock fired through every fiber, every nerve ending in her body. Even as her brain recoiled, knowing well all the arguments why they should be apart, her body responded at its own base, animal level, aroused by the proximity to her mate.

"Giovanni!"

She spun around to face him, barely able to hold back the shudder of wanting.

"I'm surprised you remember."

The flames of desire his presence sparked were doused by the chill of his tone. She needed to be in control as he so obviously was.

"What do you want?" Her voice sounded hoarse and breathless.

"I want what I paid for. Come closer, I wish to see you."

She stayed where she was.

"It was you, wasn't it? You bought out Guy."

"If that is the name of your lover who has more interest in money than loyalty then that is correct."

He walked slowly towards her.

She stepped back instinctively.

"He is not my lover." She bit her lip, angry with herself for the explanation that sprung automatically to her lips. She'd thought the days when she needed to defend herself from his jealous accusations were long gone.

He continued to advance towards her, but this time she didn't move. There was nowhere to go.

He was as stunning as ever: a killer mix of elegance, sensuality and intensity. Elegance in his Italian style: from the finely-cut clothes that flattered his tall, rangy frame to his dark hair, sharply cut, but long enough to graze his collar.

And his mouth: beautifully shaped, the lips were pressed firm as if for control. But she knew the magic they could perform.

Then she forced herself to meet his gaze: intense and unnerving. The white New Zealand light drained his eyes of their warmth, robbing them of color, leaving nothing but the darkening grey of the sky reflected back at her. Framed by the dark shadows of sleeplessness and straight, black brows, there was no sign of his restless intelligence now—only cold anger. She'd never seen him so remote, so unfeeling. Not to her anyway.

He crossed his arms and casually leaned against the wall, away from her, coolly observing her reactions but displaying none of his own. She was thankful for the slight increase in distance between them.

"I have no interest in your lovers. I have simply come to claim what's mine."

Rose jumped on his arrogant words like a lifeline, thankful for the rising anger that gave her a sense of control over the emotions that stormed within.

"You think just because we are married that you own me?"

A smile flickered across his face, quirking his lips briefly, but providing no relief to the cold certainty of his eyes.

"Your medieval notions of marriage are interesting, but not relevant. It is your business that I want and now own."

"Well, you can't have it."

"Too late. I own it."

"Not without my approval you don't." She was bluffing but it was worth a shot.

He shifted off the wall and walked around her to the desk, picking up a bunch of untidy receipts and invoices before dropping them back onto the pile.

"You were never good with paperwork were you, *cara?*"

With his back to her, she couldn't see his expression but from his voice—softer now, more casual—she knew he was at his most dangerous.

"What the hell do you mean?"

"You have nothing. It belongs to me now."

He thumbed through some of her papers.

"Leave them alone—that's private stuff." Rose snatched a contract from his hands. He turned slowly to her.

"No. It's mine now. You seem a little slow to understand. It all belongs to me now: the company, your papers. Mine."

"No. You're lying. It can't do. It's mine. I started up this company, I developed it and arranged for the finance—"

"And that was your big mistake."

And she knew it.

He plucked the paper out of her hand. She had no choice but to let him.

She rubbed her forehead with her fist in an effort to stop the pounding, to erase the events of the last ten minutes, to get her life back to where it had been. She took a deep breath but Giovanni dominated the very air that she breathed—expensive aftershave mixed with something distinctly male, uniquely him. He'd used to laugh at the way she'd snuggle into him, smelling his neck and his chest, his stomach...

She jerked her head up to face him. She couldn't weaken now.

"Why Giovanni? Why hunt me down and ruin me? What did I do to you that was so terrible?"

"You left me." His voice was low and without expression. "No-one leaves me."

She wanted to reach out to heal the hurt she detected in his lifeless tone. But there was too much that had happened since she'd been able to do that. Besides, perhaps she was wrong. Perhaps there was no hurt, only anger that she'd slipped out of his control.

"Is that it? You lost one of your possessions?"

She searched his face for a denial but found none. She saw only the changes in the features she'd once known so well. His hair was now peppered with grey. Hard lines bracketed his mouth and radiated out from his eyes. He wasn't the same man she'd once known. Strange, she thought absently, how dear and how beloved he was to her still, and yet he was also a stranger to her now: just as she'd intended him to be.

He stepped closer until they stood only an arm's length

apart. It was too close. Her breathing faltered as he lifted his hand and held her chin between his fingers.

"You've changed. I hadn't imagined that."

He frowned briefly. So briefly that Rose thought she must have imagined the accompanying flicker of sadness in his eyes.

But his touch quenched any curiosity she had as to his thoughts. It was like the soft slide of a match setting in train flames of both destruction and renewal. She felt alive for the first time since she'd left him: alive, vulnerable and raw. Pain, as strong as desire, racked her body.

She pulled his hand away from her face.

"Of course. I'm older. People age."

He held her gaze. Here, in the softer light, she could see the subtleties of his eyes—their nutmeg brown now dominated by the flecks of copper and black that darkened and cooled the heat that she'd once known within them. They had always been expressive. But now? They were more guarded and much, much colder.

"Aging is nothing. It's the fire that is no longer there."

Hurt stabbed deep within. It was true. If he'd turned cold, she'd become numb, not able or willing to feel anything.

She half-stumbled towards the window, tugging them open before he could see the hurt that both his touch and his words were causing. She needed air.

"Perhaps it's been extinguished. Anyway, I don't need fire."

He came behind her and she could feel the heat of his body close to hers, so close they were almost touching. She could feel his breath against her hair, inhaling her. She could smell his aftershave, subtle and expensive. She closed her eyes as her senses responded to everything but his touch. And it was for that, that her body yearned.

And then she felt his fingers drag a curl down her back,

testing its strength before releasing it. She held her breath, trying to control the trembling of her body, as she felt his fingers hesitate before continuing to trail down her spine. Too soon he pulled his hand away.

"Life without fire is cold, dolce mia."

He turned her around and slipped his hands up over her shoulders. He pulled her to him, his breath as hot as the Favonio wind upon her cheek, destroying the last shreds of her willpower. His eyes darkened with desire, but also narrowed with a control she didn't recognize.

"Life without passion is death," he continued, dipping his head to hers and brushing his lips against hers. Like the stimulation of silk against a skin starved of sensation, it felt erotic, enticing and thrilling.

He hesitated briefly and she could feel him inhale into her hair once more before he pulled back, his eyes searching hers for some kind of answer. A look of satisfaction spread into his eyes.

"You want me still."

She could hear the huskiness of passion in his voice: the roughness stirring her own desire even further, even as she desperately sought to control it.

"You're wrong. I don't want you."

"Then why is your body straining to mine? Why are your breasts tight with need? And why are your lips," he rubbed his thumb against them, "moist and apart, inviting me to enter them?"

He pulled her hips to his and she closed her eyes as she felt herself surrender to the madness that coursed through her body, dulling her mind with all its fears and confusion.

Then he kissed her. Not like before but with a claiming, a branding that was all about ownership. This was crazy. But it was all that she'd ever wanted. She gave in to his passion and encircled his body with her arms, drawing him closer to her.

His hands caressed her back in a feverish dream of touching —an exploration of a blind man desperate to recreate a long-forgotten vision.

She could feel his readiness for her and she wanted him to make her whole again, for her to be as one with him. Just the thought of him inside her set the muscles deep within into a shuddering spasm that emerged in a soft gasp from her mouth.

But then he pulled away. His eyes followed his fingers as they moved around her lips, under her cheekbones and up into her hair. It was the expression in his eyes as they followed the course of his fingers—an almost shocked intensity—that burned away the veil of desire.

He caught her gaze and she saw his expression harden once more. It wasn't like him. There was a control there she'd never seen before. God knows he'd needed it in the past but now he was a stranger to her.

She pulled his hand away.

"No, Giovanni. We must stop this. I need you to let me go. I have my life here and that is all I want."

"And who ever got what they wanted in life?" She felt his sadness despite his bitter tone.

"I won't give up trying. I won't give up."

He smiled a smile totally devoid of humor. "Too late. It's gone. Your future is with me now."

She shook her head. "No way Giovanni. I left you and I won't be coming back. There is no future for us."

Rose watched Giovanni's jaw tighten and grind in response.

"Haven't I made myself plain? You have no choice." The words were still smooth, but Rose could hear the steely undercurrent.

"Everyone has a choice. I made mine two years ago."

"You will come with me."

"Have I hurt your male pride Giovanni? Perhaps you should go before I destroy it altogether."

His lips hardened in a parody of a smile. "I doubt even you could do that, *cara*. Come, pack your bags and we will go."

"Stop it, just stop it, for one minute."

"You have sixty seconds."

She sat down on the couch, defeated by the physicality of his presence and the dominance of his spirit. There was no way she could fight him. He sat down opposite her, one arm settled along the top of the couch, comfortable in his ownership.

"How did you find me?"

"It was easy. It did not take long."

"You don't consider two years to be long?"

"I was not interested in finding you for a while. Why would I be? You had an affair and disappeared."

She shook her head. She knew that he'd believed that she'd had an affair. She also knew that it would do neither of them any good for her to deny it. She didn't want him to know the truth and he would never have believed her anyway.

"Besides, I had other matters, other women to occupy me. But things have changed for me and I decided to seek you out again."

The barbs about the women hit home but she ignored their pain.

"What's changed?"

"It doesn't concern you."

"You've bought my company, ruined me, demanded I return with you and say that it doesn't concern me. I think it does."

"No more questions. Suffice to say that your work will be helpful to me."

"So this is purely professional."

"As professional as doing business with one's wife can be. Anyway, your work is complementary to mine. It should be. After all, I gave you your first project, did I not?"

"And I gave you the business edge you needed. It was a fair exchange."

"And will be now."

"Not now. I can't work with anyone now."

"You should have thought of that before you welcomed this man's, Guy's, capital into your business."

She leapt up. "I had no money; I left without a cent. I needed that money to start up again."

He shrugged. "That was your choice."

She gritted her teeth. "I had no choice."

"Yes, of course. Living with me must have been impossible. But, strange, you did not seem to object too strenuously when I showered you with presents, when I gave you everything you could want in your professional life and when, at night, I explored your body to ensure you received maximum satisfaction. Yes, there was obviously no contest. You had to get away."

"Giovanni. I can't explain. It's too hard."

"You could have tried, Rose."

His quiet tones cut through her more effectively than any anger.

She jumped up and indicated the front door that still lay open.

"I can't take any more of this. Giovanni. I didn't invite you here. I don't want you here."

He didn't move.

"But I am here. And there's nothing you can do about it."

"Leave now."

"No. It's not an explanation I'm here for. Your feeble explanations, your excuses, are of no interest to me any more. What I want is your services for which I've paid. And I intend to receive them—in full."

"You may have bought my company but you haven't bought me."

He withdrew a slim sheath of papers from his pocket and dropped them on the coffee table between them.

"Check the small print. Your business partner has signed away your rights. If you don't work for me for at least six months then you will be in breach of contract. Your company will be dissolved into nothing and you will be bankrupt."

She closed her eyes briefly. She knew it but still couldn't face it. "I don't believe you."

"See for yourself."

She didn't need to. She knew how ruthless her business partner could be. He'd obviously sold her down the river. And, equally, she knew how single-minded Giovanni could be when he wanted something.

"Your company doesn't need my security system. It could develop its own."

"Not like yours. You've created the best. And I'm only interested in the best."

"What do I have to do?

"I have a plane ready to take us to Milan. You will work for me there."

"I can't do it."

"Whatever you require will be made available to you."

"But what about Alberto?"

"What about Alberto?"

She could hear the chill descend into his voice.

"I can't work with your family around, and your brother in particular."

"I think you are lying, *cara mia*. I think you want to see

my little brother. However, unfortunately he is otherwise engaged at the moment."

Rose exhaled a ragged sigh of relief. A vision of what life could be like flashed into her mind. With Alberto gone, anything was possible—until his return of course. One look at Giovanni and she could see that he'd taken her silence as confirmation that she had been hoping to see Alberto. Let him believe what he liked.

"OK. I *will* come with you Giovanni."

"I never doubted it."

"Not just because of the blackmail. Sure, I have commitments that I need to meet, but I'd meet them somehow."

"Your scholarships. Very noble, Rose. If you spent more time looking after the details of your own affairs instead of concerning yourself with girls' education, you might have succeeded in retaining your anonymity."

"The scholarships were important to me. But bankruptcy doesn't worry me. I would make money somehow and I would pay back whatever I owed. I don't need much to survive."

"So it would seem." He looked around the room with disdain. "Your *eclectic* mix of styles is born of necessity I have no doubt. So if it is not money, if it is not Alberto, what is it that makes you agree? Not that you have any other choice."

Rose could sense unease in his voice.

"Because for the first time in two years, I'm finally free of the fear that you'll find me. You're here now and I don't have to face that fear every minute of every day. I don't have to hide any more."

"You really hate me so much." His words were more of a statement than a question.

She wanted to scream at him that she loved him. She wanted to hold him and heal the hurt she could feel beneath the chill veneer. But how could she tell him she loved him, when she could never live with him again? She couldn't tell him the secret that could see him follow in his father's footsteps. It could ruin his life.

"I really hated what you and your family did to me."

"And what was that? Make you into a wealthy woman?" He paused briefly. "But, you are correct. You can hide from me no longer because I will make sure we will be together, just as your body desires. You have me now. And it is me that you want whether you know it or not."

"You are wrong Giovanni. I need no man. And as soon as those six months are up I'll return here, to my home, to New Zealand. Free, both of my fears and of you."

He stepped close enough so that she heard his words only as a whisper. "You will not last one week before you are begging me to be in your bed."

"Your arrogance does credit to your race. But, rest assured, I won't be repeating my mistake of following my instincts as I did two years ago: an impressionable girl, swept away by you and anxious to please her new family. I was born with nothing and I was never allowed to forget it. By your own admission I have changed. I won't be used again."

"Whatever passed between you and my family is history and has nothing to do with me. I simply want your business skills. If, as I imagine, you can't keep out of my bed, well, you are my wife and I will take pleasure in giving you what you desire. But, for now, I want you out of here within the hour. My plane will leave this afternoon for Italy and you will be on it."

CHAPTER 2

The plane banked steeply out of Wellington airport and Giovanni stabbed his index finger on the delete key of his computer, determined not to succumb to temptation and look across at his wife.

"Doing your own emails now?"

He raised his eyes and looked at her over his laptop. She had her "butter wouldn't melt in her mouth" look. But it would. Her mouth could raise the coolest temperature. And his temperature was never cool, despite appearances.

"Obviously."

He concentrated once more on the screen of emails highlighted in bold that awaited his attention. He normally traveled with assistants who took care of the irritating details of his business.

"I'm surprised your staff let you have a computer."

"My staff do as I say."

"They do what's best for you and, since you threw your laptop out the window, that's meant keeping computers away from you."

Giovanni frowned. This was the first time in years that he'd needed a laptop. No wonder he'd had a job finding one.

"And where are your assistants anyway? I thought they never left your side."

"There are some jobs one has to do personally."

"Like blackmailing your wife."

He felt the thump of adrenalin hit his veins. *Control*, he thought.

"I prefer to think of it as persuading my wife to return to her home."

"My home is in New Zealand."

"Not for the next six months it isn't. And, after that, we'll see…"

He left the words hanging in the air and shrugged before returning his attention to the computer.

"I return home, that's what."

She crossed her legs and looked out the window. The subject was obviously not up for discussion.

He gave up trying to understand what he was reading. Instead he stabbed his finger on the delete key once more. She was wrong. She had to be. He would keep her because she wouldn't want to leave. He'd make sure of it.

Feeling the heat of her gaze upon him, he struck the delete key repeatedly. How could such cool, blue eyes have this effect on him? It tested the control he was determined to maintain. He had to. Lack of it had cost him dearly.

"Umm."

The sound reminded him of her soft moan of contentment. But it wasn't. He sighed.

"What?"

"Interesting."

He really wasn't in the mood for such games. He was determined not to respond and continued pressing random keys in an attempt to maintain the fiction that he knew what he was doing.

The silence grew and he pressed one key too many and the program suddenly quit. He looked up, annoyed.

"And *what* is 'interesting' supposed to mean?"

One angry glance from him and people usually stopped irritating him. But his manner appeared to have no effect whatsoever on Rose, who remained composed.

"Just that you don't actually seem to be reading anything before you delete the messages. Hope they're not important."

He stopped himself from hitting the delete key once more, despite the fact the program was no longer open. God only knew what would happen if he struck the key again.

"And why would that concern you? Worried that I'm missing out on lucrative deals?" He pushed the damn computer away from him, sat back and allowed himself to gaze full and long on his wife.

Her fine features were even finer, if that were possible, and her pale skin was golden from the hot New Zealand sun. On one hand she looked stronger—tanned and lithe—and yet on the other she seemed to possess a strange quality of separateness. It was as if she'd removed herself from the world. It was in her eyes—the cool blue of a winter's sea—no longer inviting, but always challenging, repulsing now.

She was right. She had changed. The uncertain girl who would do anything to fit in, to follow her dreams of belonging, had been replaced by a woman who kept the world at arm's length.

What had made her change?

Who had made her change?

He swept the complex feelings of anger, frustration and sadness aside. He'd discover her secrets. He just needed some time. And he'd just bought that.

She shrugged her shoulders. "Your business is your own. No concern of mine."

Time he rattled her poise a little.

"Or perhaps concerned that I'd snub a lover?"

Much to his irritation she smiled sweetly at him, the sort of guileless smile, which had got him into trouble with her in the first place.

"I'm not concerned about money, lovers or anything else. Just intrigued by your change of habits."

"I am not a creature of habit. You memory is faulty on that point."

"Come on, I know how much you hate computers. Your style was always short, sharp commands—either by phone or in person. Two years couldn't have changed you that much. Unless…"

He raised his eyebrows. Why was she goading him?

"Unless what? You have some stunning revelation about me?"

"Only that my presence appears to be irritating the hell out of you and you're taking it out on a defenseless computer. I can see why you needed me in the first place with IT skills like that."

He clicked the laptop closed. "And I need you now, angelo mia." It was his turn to unnerve her. She had to learn that she was here at his insistence and on his terms. "You always were very perceptive, very sensitive to my needs." He didn't even need to move towards her to see the flush of heat pulse through her body. "I can see you haven't changed."

She turned away quickly, flicked her hair over her shoulder in a dismissive gesture and assumed an intense interest with the view outside the window.

He leaned towards her, taking the opportunity to breathe in her smell—fresh and sensual at the same time—he could never get enough of it. Then he followed her gaze as the glittering lights of Wellington city reduced to pinpricks before becoming extinguished by the darkness of the surrounding hills.

"You came as far as you could to get away from me."

Her eyes closed briefly as if struck by something in his tone rather than his words. He'd tried to keep it neutral—but he wasn't overly familiar with anything neutral.

"I needed distance. I had to get away."

"To a small country where you led a small life."

She looked at him sharply.

"You don't have to live in Europe and spend a lot of money to live a full life."

"No. But it's usual to leave the house occasionally. You lived like a hermit."

No-one else would have noticed but me, he thought: the flash of pain in her eyes, the sharp contraction in her brows and around her mouth. The hurt. It was over in a moment, covered by an affected indifference. He knew the indifference was a mask because everything else about her told him that she was anything but indifferent.

He'd succeeded in wiping the humor from her eyes and he suddenly wished he hadn't.

"I suppose there's little you don't know about my life." Her voice was flat.

"There's nothing I don't know about your life." He'd got through to her at last. He might as well continue to see how much she could take. He relaxed back into his seat. "You seldom traveled, carried out all your business online and mixed only rarely with the local community. I know everything: from who you saw, to the contents of your shopping trolley."

Rose swallowed her anger. "Must have been fascinating reading."

"Not just reading. Watching too."

"You had someone film me? That's not only an invasion of my privacy, that's plain creepy."

"Not in this day and age. Everyone is watched by someone—the government, friends, family."

"Acting a little love-sick aren't we?"

"Acting like someone who is looking after their investment."

"An investment?"

Her voice was icy; the words enunciated too clearly.

"An investment?" Rose repeated, except louder this time. Her anger was betrayed by the sharp sibilant edge she gave the word. But she was past caring—this was the last straw.

"What else would you call someone in whom one has poured money, hoping for a return. It's simple economics, Rose."

The old feelings of inadequacy came flooding back. But with it now was a strength gained through her years on her own.

"You condescending bastard. I am not an item for your balance sheet. I'm damn good at creative IT work."

"If perhaps, a little lacking in admin expertise."

The accuracy of his criticism made her see red.

"Who was it who turned your security business around? ME! But who was it who nearly knocked a million US off your balance sheet when seducing the girlfriend of your business partner?"

"Not you."

"Glad you got that one right." Rose sat back in her seat.

"Anyway, you make it sound as if it were a bad thing. The girl in question was breaking up with my partner."

"Shame she hadn't told your partner that."

He shrugged. "I don't know why you're so concerned, it was before your time."

"I'm not concerned." She said between gritted teeth. "I'm just making a point."

"Which was?"

"God knows." She slumped back in her chair. "Giovanni. Sometimes you drive me crazy."

"At last we've found something we have in common."

She sighed heavily. "I'm tired. I want to rest now."

"Rest. Sleep if you like. I have business to attend to."

As soon as her eyes were closed an image of Alberto's smoothly handsome features came to mind. Giovanni's little "investment," he'd called her.

Thank God Alberto wouldn't be in Milan. Just the thought of him made her skin crawl. At first he'd tried to seduce her but when that had failed he'd grown angry and had tried to find creative ways to humiliate her. With unerring skill he'd identified her weak points and suggested that the only reason Giovanni had married her was to protect the family's commercial interests: a useful investment for the family. Why else would Giovanni have married a nobody, far less beautiful than any of the women with whom he'd been linked?

Giovanni couldn't know of the private taunts his brother had subjected her to. Taunts that ultimately turned poisonous with abuse. But Giovanni had just used the same word.

An investment, a possession. A possession that had slipped from his grasp. Whatever Giovanni's feelings for her —if he had any—he would be angry that she'd left. One didn't just leave Giovanni Visconti. If one did, one lived to regret it. Giovanni had a way of making you pay.

And how exactly, she wondered, was he going to make her pay?

She opened her eyes once more finding no relief in her

thoughts. Giovanni's attention had returned to the computer. Why he bothered was beyond her. He didn't need to. He had enough staff to run a small country.

She turned to the blackness of the Tasman Sea—New Zealand now long gone—as they headed towards Australia. From there they'd stop briefly in Singapore and then on to Italy.

Twenty-four hours alone with Giovanni.

She guessed that it wouldn't take long to find out what exactly he had in mind.

IT WASN'T until the steward had laid out selection of Italian antipasto, together with some fresh New Zealand delicacies that Giovanni joined her at the table once more.

"A glass of champagne, Signora Visconti?" The steward's smile was warm, despite his formality.

Rose started at her old name and then smiled acceptance. But it wasn't until the door closed behind the steward that Giovanni broke the silence.

He held up his glass. "Salute."

"Are we celebrating something?"

"Our renewed partnership, *cara*."

"A *forced* partnership."

"Come, you will benefit. If only to, what was it you said, be 'free of the fear' that I will find you. The fact that I will set you up financially for the future is surely not insignificant."

"Giovanni, you seem to be ignoring the fact that I didn't choose to be here."

"Perhaps you did not think it possible?" He shrugged. "But, here we are, together at last."

She closed her eyes at his arrogance, at his inability to imagine that someone may disagree with him. She sighed, knowing when she was beaten. "Here we are…"

"Now, you must eat. You look as if you haven't eaten dinner since you left Italy."

"I guess that could be a compliment."

"It could be, but it isn't. You are too skinny. I prefer flesh on my women."

"Just as well I'm not your woman then isn't it?"

"Don't be ridiculous. You are my wife."

"In name only." She popped an oyster into her mouth, relishing its texture and the cheek-pinching tang of fresh lemon.

He sighed and let his head drop back on the seat. "You will always be my woman, whether you or I like it or not."

"I'm sure you tell all your conquests that they belong to you."

He shrugged. He looked indifferent to the fact that his image was regularly plastered over the tabloids, a new woman on his arm at every party.

"All women need to feel loved."

"Loved, but perhaps not stifled."

"You are splitting hairs. It is an excellent trait in an IT professional, but irritating in a woman." He glanced at his watch. "Eat. Then we'll get down to business. We have a day —and a night—ahead so we may as well be productive."

"And this is the night if I'm not mistaken. Surely you don't make your staff work at night?"

"But what better opportunity? We have only one bedroom."

"You have two bedrooms on this plane, Giovanni. I know, I've counted."

"You wouldn't put the staff out of a bed now would you?"

"They have their own quarters."

"Not tonight. We have a larger complement than normal. So we will be sharing a bedroom. You are my wife after all."

"In name only."

She couldn't read the complex message in his eyes.

"Eat. You'll need your strength." He pushed a plate of risotto over to her and, despite herself, her mouth watered. He was right, it had been a long time since she'd eaten such an exquisitely prepared meal.

BY THE TIME Rose had finished eating, she had also had enough of the questions.

Giovanni had eaten little during dinner, preferring to interrogate her about her time in New Zealand. To begin with she'd attempted to answer his questions. Then she'd resorted to one-syllable answers. Then, to silence.

She pushed away her empty plate and placed her elbows on the table, resting her chin on her steepled fingers

"Giovanni. I'll put this as plainly as possible. We were separated for two years and what I did, in the little time that you can't possibly have information about, is my affair. Mine. I have had enough of your jealousies."

"I was merely protecting what was mine."

"I am not your possession."

He was silent for a moment. "I know." His words were as quiet as they were shocking to her. "But I do not feel that way."

"No, you don't. And it's impossible. Do you remember at the Scala party when you hit that man for talking to me?"

"He deserved it."

"That was the first time. I should have known then that you couldn't be trusted."

He turned from her to pour more wine.

When he faced her once more his expression was cool. Her words seemed to have had no effect on him.

"Of course I hit him. He deserved it for trying to seduce

you. I don't know why you were so upset—why you left in anger."

"Because I was tired of it all."

"So you hid in the church."

"I did not 'hide'. And, anyway, I never did understand how you knew where to find me."

"Instinct. That's how I live. The church moved you once and you were drawn to it again. It was a place of refuge for you in some way." He shrugged.

She shook her head. She didn't want to admit that it wasn't a refuge—anything but—it was where she felt closest to him. Where she could remember him as he truly was: no jealousy, no issues of control. Where she could gain strength by reminding herself how much she loved him.

"It was peaceful. And it held good memories for me: of our first night together when, oddly, you decided to show me the sights. Strange, we didn't get to see any more sights after the church."

"I'd asked you to marry me. It would have been strange indeed to continue our tour of Milan after that."

"I thought you were crazy. We'd known each other for, what? Four hours?"

"It was enough."

The silence extended around them as they both remembered. It had also been silent that night in the Santa Maria presso San Satiro: a haven of calm amidst the bustle and humid warmth of a Lombard summer evening.

Even now Rose could smell the candle wax and incense that had filled the air. The scent and the jewel-like decorations were inextricably linked with her realization that she loved Giovanni, more deeply and more profoundly than she had ever have thought possible.

"It was a very special night," she admitted.

"The medieval fresco is reputed to have special powers.

Anything magical enough to make the Madonna bleed is surely powerful enough to make two people know they should be together."

"Miracles, magic—it's not the real world."

"You say that as if you do not believe in miracles."

She laughed. "Of course I don't. There are no such things. Only people fooling themselves."

"Is that what you believe we were doing? Fooling ourselves?" He leaned towards her, insisting that she look him in the eye. "*Miele*, if people have faith enough in something then it can become real. Why do you not believe this?"

Rose's mouth went dry. "Because—" The thought of her child flitted through her mind. She tried again to respond. "Because it's nonsense."

He shook his head. "My English Rose, so northern, so prosaic. You have to see it to believe it, eh?" He laughed as if the idea was ludicrous. "You have to taste it to know it for what it is."

"You can't trust what you don't believe to be real."

"Touch me. Am I not real?"

He pulled her hand roughly into his and held it tightly for a moment before dropping it back to her side.

"Am I not real, *cara mia*?" he repeated.

She nodded. "Of course you are."

"Then, you can trust in me."

She jerked back her hand. "You're twisting my words."

"Come, it's time for bed."

"For work you mean."

"Of course." He grinned that rare grin that could flip her stomach at a thousand paces.

Rose swilled the remains of her second glass of wine before swallowing it, desperately trying to calm her gathering nerves.

She'd lived with Giovanni for barely a year but during

that time, if they weren't parted through work, a day hadn't gone by without them making love at least once. The idea of them being together in a bedroom without loving each other was laughable.

But she wasn't laughing.

"You're skin is flushed." He raised his finger to her neck and dragged it down, stopping just short of her black t-shirt. "Too much wine perhaps?"

"I've had two glasses."

"The thought of being alone with your husband then?"

She contented herself with a glare.

His fingers dipped under her t-shirt and scooped out a necklace from her cleavage.

"What's this? I haven't seen it before."

He rubbed the small, intricately wrought greenstone knot between his fingers. "A present?"

She could hear the old familiar tension in his voice. She took pity on him.

"You've done your homework, you know that there were no lovers. Although it's none of your business."

The jealousy that lay like a fist in the pit of his gut uncoiled. She was correct. His informants hadn't found any trace of attachment, romantic or otherwise. Still, he wanted to hear it from her.

"I need to know everything about you. It could affect your work."

"And that's all you're interested in now."

He smiled. "So tell me about the necklace. A gift or a purchase?"

She pulled the necklace away from her body and rubbed it against her palm. "A gift. From local Maori. I worked with them a little."

"Ah, yes, your scholarships for the girls."

"Life's not easy for some people."

"I understand that the recipients never met you. It was all done online. So determined were you to avoid emotional engagement of any kind."

"What I did and how I did it is no concern of yours."

"And what would happen to these scholarships if you were to break your contract?"

He felt the full effect of her glare. "You know full well I can't afford to let that happen."

He smiled briefly at her anger. He relished her display of emotion, even if it was only anger.

"Then we will make sure your little girls are able to study. But tell me, I am curious. Why no men in your life? Did you last lover put you off?"

"Who?"

"The person you left me for."

"I—"

"Don't deny it. Why else would you leave me?"

She shook her head, whether in denial or because she refused to answer his question, he could not tell.

He paced away from her then. The thought of her with someone else made him crazy. He took a deep breath before risking turning around to face her, determined to keep his words low and controlled.

"Tell me!"

Rose shook her head again. She knew that just one word would unleash that control with devastating consequences.

"You won't tell me? Why? Trying to protect someone?"

"Yes." She held his gaze, willing him to understand that it was *him* that she was protecting: wanting him to do what he'd never been able to do before—suspend his overwhelming need to own everything about her and see beyond it—to where the truth lay.

But there was no understanding, only a scornful look that

showed her exactly how little he cared for her. It was all simply a matter of pride.

"You left me because of another man."

"Stop it, Giovanni. Stop it."

"I should never have left you alone those last six months. I knew it. But you insisted." He turned with a look of disdain on his face. "So much for your declarations of love, you probably couldn't wait to fall into someone else's arms. Shame you didn't choose your boyfriend with more care. Your feelings obviously weren't reciprocated."

"Giovanni! It wasn't like that."

"Rose, it must have been, because there is only one reason why you will not tell me the truth. And that is because I will not like it." He pushed his hands through his hair. "And, I do not like it." He turned helplessly away before facing her once more. "Go. Go to bed."

She rose and shakily walked to the bedroom. She closed the door softly behind her and climbed into cool sheets and cried like she hadn't cried since she'd left Italy.

CHAPTER 3

"*R*ose."

His voice—distant and yet penetrating—
filtered into her dream and became a part of it.

She smiled at him, searching for a response, but it was as
if he couldn't see her. He called to her again, turning his
head, searching but unable to find her. And yet she was
standing directly in front of him. So close that she could see
the panic in his eyes. But she was unable to quell it. Her voice
was dumb and her body invisible to him. Blank terror seized
her and she tried to grab his arms, tried to bring his body
against hers.

She relaxed when her arm clutched heated skin. She
could feel him. It would be all right. She leaned in against
him and could have wept with relief.

"Rose." The voice came again. "Rose, wake up, you're
dreaming."

The dream faded slowly and the reality of the low roar
of the jet filled her ears. She was still trembling with the fear
of her dream, fear of losing him. It wasn't the first time
she'd had the dream. She'd usually awoken to find herself

outside on the beach, her body chilled by the night air and sea spray.

She was suddenly aware of the warmth of his body against her cheek, of his arm around her, protecting, caressing. She cried out as the intensity of her dreams collided with the intensity of her reality. She pushed herself away from him and he let his arm drop.

"I'm sorry." She thrust one shaking hand over her face and through her hair, desperate to regain her composure.

"You cannot help your dreams, *cara mia*. Lie down again. Rest."

"Stupid," shaking her head. "Just a stupid dream."

"It must have been a bad one, you were scared of something. What was it?"

She shook her head. How could she tell him that she was scared of being nothing to him, of losing him, when that was what she'd sought two years ago when she'd left him.

"Nothing." She looked up at him suddenly. "Did I say anything when I was asleep?"

"No. And you did not sleepwalk either. Must be the first time. I used to enjoy your nightly excursions."

She felt herself blush at the memory. Embarrassment at being caught sleepwalking had always been followed swiftly by love-making, wherever she'd happened to wander.

"I'm glad someone did."

He reached out and tucked a long, curling strand of hair tidily behind her ear. "Don't tell me you didn't enjoy making love with me, Rose, because I won't believe you. You wanted me always." His eyes lazily searched her face, confident and amused. "Even now, behind this cool façade, you want me still."

"In your dreams."

"No, *cara*, in yours."

He smiled, and with his fingertips swiftly traced the curve

of her face, her cheekbone, down to her mouth. Here, his smile dropped suddenly and Rose saw the dark of his eyes widen. Her breath quickened in response. His eyes flicked up to hers and they stayed, without movement, close, but held separate by conflicting powers, like two opposing magnets.

A short sharp knock at the door broke the spell and Rose pulled herself up in the bed, away from Giovanni.

She watched as he exchanged a few words with the steward at the door before returning to a sofa in the corner of the room.

What the hell was he doing here anyway? She'd gone to bed alone under the impression that Giovanni would be staying in the main cabin. And she didn't remember pulling the duvet across herself. She was just thankful that she hadn't undressed.

She pushed the duvet off and glared across the dimly-lit cabin at Giovanni.

"How long have you been there?"

"Several hours."

"What have you been doing?"

"Watching you."

"Not the world's most exciting spectator sport."

"With you it is. I never know what you will say or do—awake or asleep. It can be very entertaining."

She glared at him.

"And, I was also thinking."

"Aren't you tired?" she asked quickly in a desperate attempt to change the subject. She really didn't want to know what he was thinking about.

"Concerned about what I might be thinking?"

"Concerned that you're tired and that I'm occupying the only available bed."

"Yes, I might have joined you but you really leave little room for guests. It's curious how someone as short as yourself can manage to spread yourself across the king-size bed, just as you used to."

"I'm accustomed to sleeping by myself. Certainly not used to being fussed over. Did you put the covers over me?"

He nodded. "The air conditioning has been turned down. You would be cold otherwise."

"I can look after myself." The words of independence sprang to her lips from habit. But it wasn't how she felt. She felt cared for, for the first time since she'd left him.

"*That* has never been in any doubt."

She sighed and relaxed back on the bed. How could she remain angry with this man when he was so damned considerate? It was enough to make her angry again.

She eyed him quizzically. "So what other things about me are in doubt?"

He stood up and walked over to her slowly—each step creating a corresponding shiver down her spine. What was it about him, she wondered, that made her *feel* so acutely. His dark eyes seemed to have such depths, such knowledge of her, that all her senses went into overdrive while her capacity for thought disappeared altogether.

"I thought I knew you well, once, but I knew little. I have been watching you, trying to understand."

Her heart thumped uncomfortably in her chest.

"There's not much to understand."

"Don't be disingenuous. I'm not interested in facile banter."

"Well," she smiled brightly at him, hoping she'd be able to deflect his serious turn of thought. "Shame. Because I'm not interested in the serious stuff."

"Then go back to sleep. You look tired still."

She swung her legs over the side of the bed, away from him.

"No, I'm fine. I haven't slept that well in a long time."

"It is because I am with you."

She grinned, despite herself. "I've missed your macho confidence."

She walked past him to pour herself a glass of water. She felt his eyes on her but willed herself not to react.

"Have you, *cara?*"

She took a long studied drink of the water.

"Don't let it go to your head. I've missed many things."

"Like?"

"Italian cheese."

"Cheese. That's it?"

He stood up, took the water from her and placed it back on the table.

"That's all I can think of at the moment."

"Would you like to know what I missed?"

She shook her head slightly and licked her lips, suddenly dry with anticipation.

"No thank you."

He cupped his hand around her cheek.

She closed her eyes, trying to keep her thoughts straight. "Giovanni. Please. You take the bed, let me get on with some work."

"Work can wait. Besides I need little sleep."

She could tell he was thinking the same thoughts as she was, by the blaze of desire in his eyes. For someone who'd needed so little sleep, they'd spent a lot of time in the bedroom.

She couldn't move. She desperately needed him to move away from her.

"So you don't want me to work. How exactly do you propose we spend the next 20 hours or so?"

He dropped his hand and she released her breath, not realizing that she'd been holding it.

"I need to know you again."

His voice sent chills down her spine. There was an uncertainty evident in the rougher tone that she'd never heard before.

Her pulse raced at the implications of his words, their ambiguity, their potential.

"Why?"

He shook his head. "No more questions."

"It can't all be on your terms. Tell me. What do you need to know about me, that you don't already?"

His brow dipped into a brief frown, his dark eyes darkening even further as if a shadow had passed over them.

"Consider it an interview—a prolonged interview. There are things I wish to know and which I will discover. We'll begin now but it won't end tonight."

"When then?"

"When I discover what I need to know."

"What the hell are you talking about?"

"It is *my* question I wish answered. Now get back into bed again."

She shivered, confused and doubtful.

"Ask me whatever it is. Let's get this over with."

"There is no rush." He moved to the phone and ordered some drinks. "We have all the time in the world."

She sat down before her legs gave way beneath her.

"That time is gone, Giovanni, don't you understand? The time for talking, for listening, for understanding—it's gone."

"You refused to talk to me before, you gave us no time. Now, here is your chance."

"A chance I don't wish to take."

"You have no choice."

A discreet knock at the door was followed by the steward bringing in drinks and snacks. He laid them out on the coffee table and left without raising his eyes or talking. He was too well trained and well paid—too used to attending to his boss in a bedroom with sundry women—to make small talk, Rose supposed. Besides, the tension in the air was palpable.

"Drink?"

She shook her head. "One question then. Just one for tonight."

He laughed, "You've misunderstood. There will be no questions. I can get my answers without questions."

"You wouldn't!"

"I wouldn't what? Touch you?" He pushed the cover back off her. "Yes, Rose, I would."

"What can you hope to gain by violence?"

"Have I ever been violent with you?"

"No. Of course not—"

"Then I suggest it's unlikely I ever will be."

"Then what question are you trying to answer? Tell me that."

"A question that only your body can answer. Not your mind, not your voice, nothing else."

Heat simmered deep inside. She gasped at the intimation, the suggestion of what he was about to do to her.

"You wouldn't take me by force."

"You are not listening to me. I am interested only in your body's responses to me, not in satisfying any physical needs of my own. No matter how pressing." He didn't smile, didn't move, simply held her gaze, watching, assessing, alert.

He put down the cup of untouched espresso and brushed her hand briefly, with the palm of his hand. The gesture had a simplicity that took her breath away. Then he withdrew his hand, leaving her own hand sensitive, aware of the lingering sense of warmth of his touch. He stood over her, watching, his gaze travelled the length of her, from her chest that, she knew, betrayed her increased heart rate and rapid breathing, to her jean-clad legs.

He walked away and flicked off the light, leaving on only

the reading light beside the bed. Its light pooled on and around only her, leaving darkness and all its unknowable potential beyond her.

There was only this moment in time, with him and her. That sense of timelessness caught and held her, stemming the questions, the things she knew she should say, the things she knew she couldn't say. He was right. Her body held her in control now. And he was, had always been, master of that.

He sat on the bed next to her. He touched her hesitantly on her hand once more. Then circled the back of her hand before increasing his grip and turning it over. He pressed his thumb into her palm briefly, but strongly, showing his strength against her softness.

She bit her lip in an effort at restraint. A shiver ran the full length of her body and she closed her eyes tight as if to contain it.

Then his hand moved to her wrist, gripping first one and then the other in one hand. Their gaze met momentarily before he pulled both her hands to his lips. He seemed to inhale them, turning and kissing her palms, before catching one in each hand and sweeping them wide, pushing her arms open, leaving her exposed.

She closed her eyes as the feel of his mouth upon her neck swept away any lingering reserve. She arched back her head and turned, the silk of his hair shifting against her lips, arousing her further.

She moved her body to be closer to him and he lay down beside her, their bodies facing but not touching. When they kissed it was as if time had melted away and their passion was as fresh and strong as the day they'd met. Except that he touched no other part of her. Chastely apart, all the focus of their needs was held in that kiss—intense and demanding.

Her body's memory responded instantly to the increas-ingly relentless pressure of his mouth by pooling heat deep within. She reached out for him, drawing her body closer to his, and wriggled against him: her breasts to his chest, no thoughts, only needing to be close, to feel the heat of his body against hers.

Then he released her, too soon. And she gasped, lifting her face to meet his once more, searching for his lips. But he smiled and pulled away, still holding her hands firmly so that she was unable to move far.

He grasped her arms above her head and fixed them with one hand while his eyes hungrily swept her body. It was as if he saw her naked, despite the fact she was still dressed in jeans and t-shirt.

He pushed the t-shirt up over her breasts, revealing her sheer bra.

Then he dropped his head down as if to kiss her but, instead, his tongue circled her nipples. She gasped and tried to reach for his head, to draw him closer, to feel him more intensely, but his grip remained firm. He paused, as if to gauge her—or perhaps his—reaction before he descended once more, this time flicking the bra open with one swift movement and sucking her nipples, first one then the other, with slow deliberation. Her whole body reeled with shocked pleasure as his mouth made direct connection with the spiraling need deep inside. Her hips jerked up to meet his with each fierce suck.

Then he stopped.

She opened her eyes briefly and wished she hadn't. She'd expected to see the self satisfaction of a man who'd got what he wanted, who knew that he could take whatever he liked. But it wasn't there. All she could see was raw need, masked with a hard expression: his mouth tight, his eyes black.

Then his face dipped once more and she was pushed beyond thought, reveling in the tensions that clenched her stomach with raw lust. She opened her mouth, wanting him on her more completely.

"Please..."

He looked up then and shook his head, before moving down to kiss her stomach, as his hands unzipped her jeans. She lifted her hips and he pushed the jeans down, taking her panties with them, the white lace caught inside the rough fabric. He sat back and pulled them completely off before dropping them on to the floor. His hands swept slowly—too slowly—up her legs, his pressure increasing along with her need until she wanted to scream.

She reached down and clutched the crisp folds of his shirt, urging him upwards. As guarded as before, he moved his head slightly to one side, as if questioning. But what? What did he want of her?

She knew what she wanted of him.

Her heart was racing. She should stop but she couldn't. He was the man who'd filled her dreams, night after night, holding her, touching her, soaking her with her arousal as he rode her into oblivion. She had no choice about her dreams and she had no choice now.

"Giovanni," she said softly, calling to him, as she had so many times in the past.

She felt, rather than heard, his groan as his hands curved around her bottom before pulling her to his mouth.

Her legs jerked as his lips connected with the point where the need that clawed within, surfaced.

The tenderness had gone from his lips now. There was an urgency about his touch which her body needed. A moan escaped her lips as the tension built within her. With each flick of his tongue, each suck of his mouth, she wriggled against him, desperate for release. Her breathing quickened and she pushed her fingers into his hair, holding him there, still wanting more.

He lifted his head and looked into her eyes, dark with desire. Her hands stretched down to his body, wanting him where he should be, inside her. He grabbed her hands in one of his and shook his head. His gaze continued to hold hers as he flicked his fingers through her wetness, teasing, watching, until she could hold it in no longer.

As she cried out, his fingers plunged inside her, deepening her orgasm, sending her into an exquisite darkness and suspending her there, but only momentarily. For after the darkness came the light, and consciousness once more.

She stretched her head to one side, away from him, trying to hide from him the emotions that were playing out savagely inside. But he cupped her face with his hand and pulled her towards him until they were only a breath away from each other.

Her body trembled involuntarily as he withdrew first his fingers, then his hand and then his body. He hesitated briefly, lying close to her, as if waiting, watching.

"Giovanni," she whispered. "Come to me?" It should have been a statement but her drift back into reality had turned it into a question.

She touched his arm lightly, willing him to lose that deadly, unaccustomed control and take her fully, make them both whole again.

She could feel their breaths mingle, could see the drum beat pulse in his neck under the dark shadow of stubble. There was so little space between them, but even that was unbearable.

He shook his head. "No, *cara*. I will not."

"But, why?" She searched his face. "You don't want me?"

He smiled wryly. "Because I do not wish to."

Rose retreated as if struck. He didn't want her.

It was as if a chill wind swept over her, leaving her feeling clammy and sick.

"So that's it then?"

"I gave you pleasure is that not enough?"

He turned away from her and she shook her head in disbelief as he rose from the bed, all control once more. Receiving pleasure was never enough. How could he think it was? Did he really believe that she was a heartless woman for whom her own pleasure was paramount? If he did, he didn't know her at all.

She watched as he pulled the knot out of his tie and flung it onto the couch.

"So you're not coming to bed?"

He shook his head. "No. I'll leave you to sleep."

Realization hit her then, followed by a wave of desolation. She lay back, suddenly exhausted.

"You've done what you set out to do, tonight, haven't you?"

"Si."

"I've answered your question?"

He shook his head and smiled grimly.

"I was never asking *you* the question. I was asking myself. I have my answer."

HE CLOSED the door to the cabin and stood before the window, watching the first soft blush of dawn fill the cloudless sky, illuminating the cabin, bringing him back to this point in time. Back to the point in his life where he'd needed to know whether she was like all the others he'd had since she'd left.

He remembered waking up with his last lover, only weeks previously, and feeling nothing. His physical needs were only ever temporarily satisfied. The hunger always yawned deep inside afterwards. It was always present. He'd wanted to see if he could fill that hunger, even without satisfying himself physically. He'd wanted to be with Rose again to see if he really had experienced that with her, or whether he'd somehow imagined it.

He'd wanted to feel her, to experience her without distractions. Wanted to see if he could forget himself in her.

And he had.

There could be no-one else for him now.

CHAPTER 4

The Palazzo Visconti—home to the Visconti family for centuries and herself for a year—was buried in a leafy street in the historic centre of Milan. It had also been the place where she'd experienced her last, nightmarish, encounter with Alberto Visconti, Giovanni's younger brother. A nightmare whose consequences both she and Giovanni had had to live with ever since; he, without even knowing its cause. And she could do nothing about it.

A shiver of revulsion shook her body as she entered the marble-floored foyer: as cold and as lifeless as a museum, despite its treasures. Once the door was closed the life of the city—the shouts of the street hawkers, thud of distant music and roar of the traffic—was extinguished. Even the soft light of a misty Milan morning failed to inject its usual magic into the room. Instead the glow from the polished silver was muted and the light that managed to filter between the heavy swags of curtains was gloomy.

"Home sweet home," Rose muttered, noticing that nothing had changed, from the highly polished antiques to the massive medieval tapestry that hung along the rear wall, whose rich colors echoed the priceless carpets. It was beautiful but she'd never been comfortable here. Especially now.

"*Bentornata, mia cara.* Welcome back to where you belong."

She felt irritation prickle at his sense of ownership.

"It's your home, Giovanni, not mine any more. I'll find an apartment as soon as I can."

"No you won't. I've bought your time, 24-7. However many hours I require, you will be available to me."

"Is that right? So when you bought my company—and my time—I somehow lost all my human rights."

"Si. If you wish to look at it like that."

"I can't see how else you can interpret it. But, for your information, my days and evenings you can have—my nights are my own, on my own."

She turned away. She didn't want a response. Truth was, she was frustrated to find herself voicing the exact opposite of what she wanted.

The clanking and mechanical whirring of the ancient lift began as the rickety contraption made its way up from the basement.

"I've arranged for you to use the attic suite. You'll be more comfortable there."

She crossed her arms defensively as she waited for the lift. Was she really so easy to read? The attic suite was the only place she'd been able to re-decorate; the only place where she felt truly at home.

"In the old servants' quarters. Yes, I should think I'll feel quite at home. I guess it's been redecorated by now."

"No."

"You probably haven't even been up there since I left. No doubt your mother's re-styled it."

"It is still as you left it."

"How do you know? You go up there sometimes?"

"Rarely now."

It had been their escape. Nominally a guest suite, but more often used as her study and their private hideaway. Tucked up in the eaves—all light and simplicity—it was a place where they could talk, love and simply *be*, in private. It was a place of peace: a peace, it seemed, which Giovanni no longer sought.

Once inside the ancient lift he slammed the grille door shut and pressed the button. It didn't move.

"Hey, let's walk. This thing gives me the creeps."

He pressed the lift again. "We can't. It's the only access at present. The stairs to the attic are dangerous—I'm having them rebuilt." He pressed it again and at last something registered in the depths of the basement and the lift stuttered into life.

"You really need to overhaul this old place."

"The family likes it as it is."

Rose had forgotten the snobbery of Giovanni's family about new things. They considered anything new to be, by definition, vulgar. The only way Giovanni had been able to drag his family and its cash kicking and screaming into the world of commerce was by keeping control solely in the hands of the family. A measure he'd come to regret. But it had resulted in a billion-dollar business that kept everyone happy.

The Palazzo had been divided into separate wings for individual family members. But, since the death of his father, Giovanni, as eldest son, occupied the main part with its ornate reception rooms, soaring ceilings and irreplaceable artworks. His mother and brother occupied the other wings, while having access to the main house also.

The attic guest suite was untouched. It was the only room that she'd had carte blanche on decorating. She'd had the old-fashioned trappings stripped from the room, leaving it simple, both in terms of texture and color, making the most of the huge attic windows and revealing its glorious soaring wooden beams. The rest of the family had no interest in an attic room where once servants had slept. And that had been fine with Rose who'd used to retreat there when Giovanni had been away on business.

By habit, Rose walked directly across to the windows that she'd had enlarged. She stepped out on to the small balcony and looked over to where the turrets of an old palace—now a museum—rose. The small bronze clock on the principal turret chimed the hour. It was ten in the morning. And for the first time Rose felt a sense of inevitability: as though she were in the right place at the right time.

She turned to look at Giovanni. He hadn't moved: still stood by the door watching her.

"It's fine. I'll stay."

"That was never in doubt. It's your room after all."

"And nothing's changed in two years."

"Everything's changed, *cara*. Always. Time does not stand still."

"It looks as if time's stood still here."

"No. The room had been neglected, forgotten about."

Like me, she thought.

"I had the staff clean it up."

She turned to survey the scene outside the window once more. She pressed her lips together in an effort to suppress the feelings of sadness his words evoked.

How much had he forgotten about her? How much had Giovanni's feelings for her changed? Because one thing was certain, her feelings for him were as strong as ever.

"Rest now. There is a meeting after lunch you will attend."

"Will I?"

"If you want to keep those girls in scholarships on the other side of the world, yes you will."

"Have I told you recently what a bastard you are?"

"Last night, if my memory is correct."

"Good," she nodded satisfied. "Just wanted to make sure."

"And don't be late."

"Me? Late?"

"You are always late."

"What time is the meeting?"

"1.00 pm."

"The meeting's at 2.00 isn't it? You tell me an hour earlier to make sure I'm on time."

He nodded, unsmiling. The heavy door closed behind him and she listened as his footsteps rang on the marble floor, just as his words rang in her head.

Everything changes.

It was hard to believe that Giovanni's love for her had gone. But he seemed to be making that very clear. First on the plane—he was playing with her, determined to show her that she was as much under his spell as ever, showing her how vulnerable she was to him, how under his control she was still. He was showing her, clearly and unequivocally, that he felt nothing for her. Not even enough to make love to her.

Everything changes.

It sounded like a death knell in her head.

She balled a fist and rubbed her forehead, trying to wipe the sound from her mind.

Why the hell couldn't he have left her in New Zealand if she meant so little to him?

She turned on the shower in the bathroom and let it run until it was hot. It was only when she was naked and feeling the full force of the water on her body that the tears came. With the sound of the shower, the locked door and nowhere else to run, she let forth the flood of emotions that had been churning within her since Giovanni had arrived at her home and turned her calm little world on its head.

She braced her hands against the cool stone tiles and sobbed, letting the water run through her hair, and mingle with the tears of loss.

ROSE EMERGED from the shower feeling a different woman.

Everything changes.

Well, so it might. But there was also hope in those words: possibility, potential. Three things were certain, she still loved Giovanni, Alberto was nowhere around and she had the next six months with Giovanni.

Giovanni thought he was in control of her over the next six months. But he wasn't. He might not want her but she wanted him. And she'd do everything she could to have him. She'd done it once, surely she could do it again? If all she had was the next six months she'd make them six memorable months.

She *would* have Giovanni in her bed.

Sunlight poured through the huge windows and the smells and sounds of Italy floated in to her on the soft breeze. She felt the atmosphere of Milan surround her and she breathed deeply of it, of him.

She wanted him and she would show him that she was as strong as he when it came to getting what she wanted.

With each smooth sweep of the hair straightener, Rose felt herself change. Gone were the casual clothes and curly hair that signaled the passive, quiet life she'd lived in New Zealand.

She dressed in a beautifully cut silk shift dress—one of the many items of clothing she'd left behind that still hung in the wardrobe—and looked at herself in the mirror.

It was a very different Rose who looked back at her: business-like, cool and very, very determined. Superficial changes maybe, but they signaled the deep shift that she felt within.

She checked the time on her cell phone. She'd have enough time to make a brief diversion.

～

THE TAXI DREW up at the small cemetery on the edge of the city. Sitting astride a small hill, it overlooked the high-rise blocks and buzz of the city. Cars, bumper to bumper, crawled through the streets; trains sped, straight as a die, along the flat plain of the River Po out of the city and shifting waves of people moved everywhere in between.

But she wasn't here to look at the view. She turned back to the rows of gravestones, some new, others old and bent, their markings lost in time.

Cicadas crackled in the mid-day heat on the unshaded gravestones, a throbbing in the air that held a heavy sadness.

Rose looked around, trying to gain her bearings. She'd been there only once and her heart pounded with anxiety. What if she couldn't find it? She walked further into the cemetery, under an avenue of huge, light-flickering lime trees that provided shade to those who continued to mourn, shade for Rose. At the end of the avenue she turned up to a ridge that looked across the haze to the distant Alps. And she found what she was looking for.

The grave of her daughter.

Rose dropped to her knees and plucked away the grass that had spread over it, brushing off the dirt with her bare hands.

A gravestone for the baby she lost before full term was unusual, but she'd insisted and had made the necessary bribes. She needed to know that her child had existed and would not be forgotten. It remained a focus for her grieving, even from a distance of thousands of miles.

Carina—much loved and forever missed.

Not a day had passed without feeling her absence. The hardest times were when she'd awoken in joy after vivid dreams of holding her daughter close to her—so close that she could feel the heat of her body against hers, the sweet smell of her and her hungry mouth searching for her breast —only to find they were but dreams. Those times were hard.

Rose stayed only five minutes, not really speaking, not really thinking, just feeling close to her child.

A stillborn baby of 36 weeks, Carina should have been old enough to survive outside her mother's womb. But she hadn't and Rose hadn't been able to sustain her within it, hadn't been able to protect her from Alberto's brutal attack.

She'd kept the pregnancy a secret from Giovanni. It wasn't so hard as they'd been separated by their work for six months: he in the US and she in Hong Kong. Both had been important jobs and full on. If he'd known she was pregnant, there would have been no way he'd have allowed her to work and no way he would have been apart from her. And she hadn't wanted that. The decision had cost her more than she'd ever imagined. So, he'd never known about Carina.

But Carina was his baby too. She felt guilt at his not knowing, but she couldn't indulge herself in the truth. She had to be the strong one because, despite all of Giovanni's strength, she couldn't trust him to be strong enough not to kill Alberto. Rumors abounded about his father's violent past, a past Giovanni was terrified of repeating in his own life. And Rose couldn't trust that his passions wouldn't twist into violence with such provocation. She knew him. She knew his passion was his weakness—just as he did.

. . .

HER VISIT to her daughter's grave calmed her in a way that she hadn't imagined. She felt more peaceful than she had done in a long time when she walked up to the formal boardroom where the receptionist assured her that she was expected.

"Signora Visconti! Welcome back."

"Thank you Allegra. It's good to be back. Is the meeting ready for me?"

"Not yet Signora. Signore Visconti will invite you in at 2.30."

Rose smiled to herself as she noted the time on the clock —2.15. OK, he'd got her there.

"Any papers I should see? Not sure what this meeting's about. Any ideas?"

Allegra smiled discreetly. "You will find out in due course. Signore Visconti asked that you wait here until he invites you in."

Rose raised her eyebrows. Cloak and dagger stuff. That wasn't usually Giovanni's style. What was he up to?

She pushed aside the lifestyle magazines and plucked out a recent copy of the Economist. Rose had never been interested in trivia. She'd had too much to do all her life. She'd had to work twice as hard as any of her friends whose families supported them financially. Two part-time jobs had to be fitted around her university studies and she still felt ill at ease when she had nothing to do.

After half an hour of re-reading the same paragraph, she gave up. It was now 2.45 and she still hadn't been invited in. What was going on?"

Rose cast a surreptitious look at the door to the AV room that adjoined the boardroom. It had a projection window through which she would be able to see what was going on.

It was positioned behind Allegra's desk. For added security, only Allegra held the swipe card needed to gain access.

But Rose happened to know that Allegra had had a spare one made for the AV staff if she happened to be on one of her long lunches. It was kept in the drawer. She'd used it herself. All she needed was a few moments.

She winced, in what she hoped looked like an expression of pain. "Allegra, I couldn't trouble you for a glass of water and some aspirins could I? I've got a headache."

Allegra smiled, glanced worriedly to the conference room, but agreed. "Senz'altro."

Within moments Rose was in the AV room. She felt vaguely uneasy but justified her deception in view of the fact that Giovanni had kept her in the dark. Something was going on and she needed to know what she was about to walk into.

The first thing she saw was Giovanni's mother sitting opposite.

Giovanni had total control of his family's company but had always made sure his mother's wishes were consulted on business. It had always puzzled Rose, given her mother's obvious antagonism towards Giovanni.

The window was darkened, so Signora Visconti couldn't see Rose. But Rose could see that something was riling her. Rose switched on one of the sound controls so she could hear.

"Are you saying you don't trust the family Giovanni?"

"No."

He had his back to the window but Rose could see, by the way he sat, that he was in command of the situation, as usual. But there was no sense of relaxation: his body was held stiffly. He might be in control of the meeting but he was also a little on edge.

"It's a standard IT security system and the contract you have before you is simply to engage the services of a consultant to undertake security checks and install IT security for all the Visconti holdings. Surely you want our investments secure?"

"Yes of course. But I'm not happy about it."

I bet you're not, thought Rose. Both she and Giovanni were aware that his mother treated her family's business as her personal bank account. There was nothing extravagant in her dealings and Giovanni didn't mind, just as long as they continued to remain transparent.

"Nevertheless, I think we should proceed. But I would like your agreement."

"This has always been a family business Giovanni. I'm not happy for outsiders to be raking through our computer files and accounts. No. It should wait until we are able to undertake this work ourselves, in the family. Alberto will return in a few months. A family member is what we need."

Giovanni turned to the secretary of the company. "Please ensure the minute clearly states Signora Visconti—senior's—agreement to proceed providing the work is carried out by a family member."

He checked the minutes. "Good. All agreed?"

His mother inclined her head in agreement.

"Well, if there is no further business, I'll leave." Giovanni's mother rose from her table before Giovanni stopped her.

"One moment." He reached for the telephone.

Rose slipped past a bewildered Allegra and entered the boardroom, all nerves forgotten by the scene she'd witnessed and the clash of feelings that it had engendered.

Rarely had Rose encountered such a hush in a room—the sort of quiet that felt heavy with unspoken thoughts. But the look on her mother-in-law's face was priceless.

Ignoring her, Rose strode past her to the seat Giovanni indicated on his right-hand side.

Sparked out of silent amazement at the sudden reappearance of their boss's long-lost wife, members of the executive team muttered their greetings.

Rose swung into her chair, ran her hands across the smooth grain of the board table and smiled generally in acknowledgement.

"Gentleman," she smiled. "Signora Visconti," she nodded in cool acknowledgement. She felt no inclination to smile at her mother-in-law. The woman had done her best to make her life miserable when she'd lived in Milan.

Giovanni's mother rose from her seat slowly as if movement was difficult, her eyes focused solely on Rose. "Giovanni," she still didn't look at him. "What is this woman doing here?"

"Mother, my wife has kindly agreed to carry out the necessary security work. She has an international reputation in the field, as you are all no doubt aware." He scanned the room observing who was nodding in agreement and who looked as uncomfortable as his mother. "Also, of course, she is a member of our family and so ideally placed to run the project."

"And do you, *signora*, have anything to say about this?"

Her mother-in-law's expression could have frozen a lesser person. But Rose knew her well and disliked her intensely. Not least for how she treated Giovanni.

Rose turned to the others. "Thank you for your welcome. It's been a long time but I'm glad to be back and looking forward to working with you all."

"Giovanni. We will discuss this."

"Madre, we've already discussed this and agreed upon a course of action. Rose will take it from here." He pushed his chair from the table and stood up. "Signora Rose Visconti will report directly to me for the duration of her contract and will provide a report to the Board upon completion."

"And when will that be? How long will we have to put up with this slut amongst us again?"

Slut? That was a new insult. She'd called her many things during her time with Giovanni but she'd never suggested that she'd had lovers. There would have been no point. Rose and Giovanni were rarely apart—rarely alone maybe—but always together, except for those last months before she'd left.

The silence was even heavier than before. Rose was sure that the other executives would have loved to have dropped through the floor, escaped as best they could, so used were they to the Giovanni's explosive temper. But they sat transfixed, like rabbits in a car's headlights.

Rose didn't dare look at Giovanni. But she could see his temper spark in the movement of his fingers, flicking straight and then curling tightly, trying to hold in the anger. What the hell was he going to say?

She saw him take a deep breath and then look to his team.

"The meeting has concluded. Signora Visconti will report her findings within six months."

There was a quiet gasp of astonishment from the executives as they left the room as quickly as they could.

Rose knew that they weren't surprised at the project, at her appointment or its report date. No, it was Giovanni's reaction that had them flummoxed—and her.

"Rose," he indicated that she should precede him.

She smiled tightly and walked on through to his office. She stood, arms folded, looking out the window, across the city to the vast plains beyond and waited for the door to close behind him.

"Thanks for telling me, Giovanni."

"Thank you for taking it so well, Rose."

"I am not taking it well. I'm furious."

"Why? It is your specialty. Perhaps I had not told you all the details."

"Yes, you'd omitted to tell me that you were pitching me against your mother. God, Giovanni, she hates me enough already for taking her beloved son away from the family."

"Not a beloved son, merely her most useful. I wouldn't have thought my mother's enmity would matter to you."

"It doesn't. But that's not to say I like it."

"Then why your anger?"

"Because, I…" She sighed heavily and dragged the hair off her face as she paced the floor.

"Perhaps because you really did not expect there to be business to be done. Perhaps you thought I was using business as a pretext to lure you back to Milan, back to my bed. Is that why you're angry? Because you thought it was personal and it's not?"

Why indeed? He'd plainly told her that the only reason he'd sought her out was for business. But he'd made her believe it was personal. And it wasn't.

"I would have been a fool to believe it was personal."

"And you are no fool. That is why I need you."

She closed her eyes briefly as a defense against his words, against the meaning that he so obviously wasn't expressing, and that she wished he was.

"You could buy anyone."

"Who better than you? You have the creativity, the IT skills, you are a member of the family. But, most of all, it is your lack of trust in everyone and everything that is required here."

His words hit home as she was sure they were meant to; all the more for their veracity.

She turned slowly to face him. "I trust where it's earned. I just haven't found anyone who's earned it yet."

"For your sake, I hope one day you do." He looked down

suddenly and flicked through some papers before pushing them across the desk to her. "Here, you've some reading to do."

"You and I need to talk some more first. There are things you aren't telling me and I doubt that I'll get from any document. What's behind all this security work?"

"You need no further information. Prior knowledge may influence your work. Just do a thorough job."

"Don't I always?"

"You are thorough in everything, *cara*. Even, in covering your tracks."

"But you still found me."

"Because I have power and you do not."

"Not over me you don't."

"Wrong. For the moment I do. Complete you work and then you can go."

"It will only take me a few months."

"Then you will be able to leave earlier than the six months. I'll amend the contract. Just do the work, Rose. Comb the records for inconsistencies, set the traps and find any culprits. With proof. That is all. I will see you later at dinner."

"Dismissed, am I? Is that how you dismiss your wife?"

"No. That is how I dismiss an employee."

"I am not your employee in the strictest sense of the word."

"In whatever sense you care to name you appear to be irritated that, as far as I am concerned, our relationship is strictly business."

"And you, signore, are too conceited to believe that I am perfectly happy with a business arrangement."

She scooped up the papers and walked out the door, trying hard not to notice the fact that he was smiling.

. . .

HE SAT THERE for some time watching the door through which she'd just exited, amused by her ability to deceive herself.

He rarely lied. But, in this instance, it was required if he was to get Rose back where she belonged—with him, permanently.

He needed a job doing. He needed to find evidence of Alberto's pilfering. And he needed it done well and with discretion. But he needed something more.

He needed to show her that he'd changed. He wanted to show her that he would never again allow his jealous, possessive nature to run out of control. He wanted her to see that he could let her leave his office without his hands tracing the soft blush of anger on her cheek, without his lips persuading her lips to release the tight anger he could see there and to swell into soft submission.

It seemed Alberto had been correct.

That night, two years ago, when Rose had failed to turn up to meet him when he'd returned to Milan, he'd found only Alberto and a story that he'd had no choice but to believe.

Alberto had described how Rose had come to him complaining of the way Giovanni stifled her, of how she needed someone who could think like her, who could love like her—a cool, northern love that was subtle, refined. A love that she thought she could find in the blonde Alberto. According to Alberto, he'd repulsed her advances and she'd left.

Giovanni's pain had overtaken his sense at the time.

Devastated, he'd not questioned Alberto, knowing in his heart that the accusations were true: he *was* demanding, he *was* emotional, he *was* possessive. And Rose hadn't been able to take it any more. In the last few months before she'd left, she'd become evasive in their phone calls, not answering him directly. She'd avoided meeting up with him during their enforced separation. He'd been suspicious, wondering what it was she was covering up. It had all seemed to fit with Alberto's story. She'd wanted Alberto; she'd been rejected and she'd left, unable to face Giovanni any longer.

He didn't doubt that someone could want and love Alberto more than they loved him. It had always been that way with his parents. Rose had fallen for Alberto, just as he'd always feared.

But it wasn't just Alberto's testimony, some of his own staff had back up Alberto's story.

Damning, convincing and devastating. Until that night only a few weeks ago when he'd met up, by chance, an old friend of Rose's who asked after her child.

Whose child was it? His? Alberto's?

That Alberto had been lying about spurning her advances, he was sure. No-one could refuse his Rose anything. Least of all his brother who had no morality whatsoever.

Could she have been pregnant with Alberto's child and lost it? Is that why she'd left him? Too ashamed to return, rejected by Alberto when he'd learned of the child, and likely to be spurned by the jealous Giovanni?

After he'd spent the evening with Rose's friend, trying to glean as much information as possible, Giovanni had walked home, oblivious to everything except the fact that Rose could have been in pain, needing him and he hadn't been there for her.

The thought hadn't left him over the following week. Making love, drinking heavily, work—nothing could expunge it. All he could think of was Rose: vulnerable beneath that unemotional façade, hidden from herself as much as from the world, alone.

It had taken only days to find her and even less time to organize the finer details. All he needed now was for her to tell him the truth but for that he needed to earn her trust. He needed to show her that he could control his jealous, passionate nature for her sake. Words wouldn't do it this time.

He rubbed his eyes. He was tired; he was impatient but there was too much at stake to rush her. To earn her trust she needed time and space. He could afford to give her a little of both.

CHAPTER 5

*A*fter Giovanni had briefed Rose's team, there was an exchange of baffled looks at Rose's sudden reappearance. The status of Giovanni's and Rose's relationship remained unexplained and Rose certainly wasn't going to enlighten them—not when she didn't have a clue herself.

She spent the afternoon with her team in meetings discussing the new security systems she'd devised and how they'd be implemented. They'd be working closely together but she'd do the one-off investigation, have overall control and only she would know the identity of anyone found implicated in illegal transactions. Giovanni had insisted.

The rest of the day passed in a whirl of meetings, culminating with a presentation to Giovanni of their plans. Giovanni listened to Rose's presentation with an uncharacteristic, inscrutable expression. He didn't say a word as she described the details of the overall aim and functionality of the project down to the creative strategies. Luckily, her professionalism was faultless, despite Giovanni's unnerving attitude, and he appeared satisfied. With a flick of his hand they were all dismissed, including her.

She pulled together her papers and smiled at her team, trying hard to keep the hurt at bay.

It wasn't until early evening that she closed down the laptop and called it a day. She stretched, yawning. Jet lag was catching up with her.

The office was deserted and she headed for the elevator.

As she exited the building, a car pulled up alongside. Simon, Giovanni's assistant jumped out.

"Signora?" He held the door open.

"No thanks, Simon. I need some air." She smiled and continued to walk on.

But he merely slammed the car door shut and fell into step with her as the car crawled beside them.

"Signore Visconti would like a few words."

She stopped walking abruptly. "Would he now?"

Simon smiled and nodded diplomatically. He never elaborated, always said the minimum. Rose knew from old that there would be no information forthcoming from Simon about his boss. He was both devoted and discreet.

She bent down and peered inside the shaded interior before turning back to Simon. "I take it Signore Giovanni is too busy to ask me himself."

"Signore Visconti is working."

Simon opened the door and Rose got into the car next to Giovanni who was talking on his phone.

He barely acknowledged her as they drove off, stopping and starting through the rush-hour traffic.

She looked out the window and listened to the stream of Italian and the deep timbre of his voice. Her stomach clenched with desire.

He flicked the phone shut suddenly—without any niceties, abrupt and final.

"You really should learn how to say goodbye nicely, Giovanni. It's only polite."

He angled his body to hers and hooked one arm across the back seat, grazing her hair with his hand.

"And you'd know all about that, wouldn't you?"

She looked at him sharply. "That was different."

"Ah yes, it's always different, always a special case when it comes to yourself, isn't it?"

"It certainly appears to be. I don't know many people whose husbands rob them of their company and money and force them to return to them against their will, despite the fact they have no future together.

"Their men must be weak."

"Their men are normal."

He laughed, harsh and short.

"If you'd wanted normal you should have stayed in London amongst your own people." He lifted his hands and pulled back a shaft of hair that fell over her shoulder. "But you didn't, did you? You wanted more."

"You're wrong. I want what every woman wants."

"And that is?"

She grimaced. She wasn't going to admit what she wanted to him. What was the point?

"You don't need to tell me," he continued. "You want a man of passion when it suits you—in the bedroom—and a man without the inconvenience of passion outside the bedroom."

"Sounds good to me."

"Ah, but the catch is that you cannot have both. Which do you want most, I wonder?"

He brought his finger to her lips before she could reply. "Don't worry. It will be the latter. Our bedrooms are separate; there will be no inconvenient passion to disturb your days—or nights."

She closed her eyes briefly against the frustration. He must know that she wanted his passion more than anything.

His jealousies and controlling behavior seemed nothing to her now.

"I see the thought that I do not insist you lie with me relieves you."

"As if you could insist."

He leaned in to her. "You know I could, dolce cuore. And not by insisting. Rather by persuasion. But I choose not to."

"So why are you chauffeuring me from the office to the Palazzo? Think your wife might be led astray by an amorous Italian?"

She could see the barb found its mark but he recovered quickly. "It is always wise to protect one's investment," he smiled lightly. "Otherwise it ceases to have value."

She glared at him.

"And what exactly is it that you want from your investment at this moment?"

"I want your assurance that your work remains completely confidential. I don't want names mentioned to your team; I don't want specific findings revealed. They must only ever know a small piece of the whole. It will be only you who knows the full picture. I need your assurance on this."

Surprised, she nodded. "That's standard. Why the secrecy?"

"The 'why' is not your concern. Simply do your job, fulfill your contract and then you will be free once more. Just as you wish to be."

"Fine."

As they pulled up outside the Palazzo, Rose didn't wait for Simon and turned to let herself out of the car.

"And, Rose, don't wait up, I doubt I'll be home for dinner."

She jumped out without a backward glance.

∾

ROSE LOOKED down the length of the rosewood table at the antique grandfather clock that mournfully chimed two long strokes—wrong, as usual—and sipped her glass of wine.

Apart from those last few months, she couldn't remember a time when Giovanni had not spent the evening with her. More often than not, business had to be mixed with pleasure, but it had never taken precedence before.

Times had changed, obviously. She would be dining alone.

She shook out her napkin, helped herself to dinner and looked around the oppressive room.

Alone, surrounded by the ornate paintings of his ancestors, Rose felt suffocated by the weight of his family's history. Her eyes ranged from the older paintings depicting grim-faced ancestors to the modern-day paintings of Giovanni's own family.

The artist had caught Giovanni's strength and pride but not his passion: that, even the finest artist had been unable to convey.

Her eyes shifted to his brother—his only sibling. There, the artist had been more successful. Alberto's eyes gazed upon the watcher with a bored, sardonic humor. His full upper lip was curled slightly as if irritated by the whole exercise. It was the face of a spoilt young man, with more ambition than ability.

Her heart thumped uncomfortably in her chest and she studied her wine as she tried to calm herself. Alberto wasn't here. Apparently wasn't even due back until well after her contract expired. Without him, things could continue as they were before. She could plan her future, back in New Zealand, and make her escape before his return. She loved Giovanni and it was for his sake that she needed to leave before Alberto returned.

Because she wouldn't be able to hide from Giovanni the

fact that his brother had attacked her in an attempt to rape her, destroying their baby in the process. And she didn't know whether he'd be able to control his rage at her hurt. What if his worst fears came to pass and he attacked his brother, just as his father had when he'd nearly killed a man? She daren't risk him discovering her secret, risk his passionate rage that might know no bounds.

She took another mouthful of food and studiously avoided looking at Giovanni's portrait.

How could she have let herself fall back into his life again? Her love for him had continued unabated, but his passion for her had been like a distress flare—powerful, lighting up her whole life, but, seemingly, quick to extinguish.

And here she was, loving him, wanting him, but leaving him quite untouched. There was nothing but coolness from him now.

What she'd give to see that heat once more.

She sipped from her glass of wine, pushed back the half-eaten plate of food, and wondered where he was and what he was doing.

It wasn't like him. They'd always made sure that everything stopped for their time together. But not now. And how could she expect otherwise? She'd left him believing that she'd had enough of his over-the-top passions that reminded her of the histrionics of her unstable mother.

A man with his pride would never forgive her. He was probably out now with one of the many young, beautiful Italian women that flocked around him in the up-market restaurants and clubs that he frequented. Yes, she could just see it: blonde hair flicked artfully to one side and head inclined slightly as the woman listened to him, the accidental graze of her hand upon his thigh, shifting in her seat as she indicated her receptiveness to his sexuality.

She sat back in the chair, shook her head and groaned.

He'd been right. She *was* disappointed because he'd wanted her for the work, rather than for anything else. She suddenly realized the depth of her need for him. Perhaps she should track him down and flirt with him, make him see what he was missing. Make him see her as a woman, not a business colleague. Then it occurred to her. She wouldn't need to track him down. She could use his jealousy for once and lure him to her. She'd go to the club that was his second home. Giovanni would be told in minutes that she was there.

IT WAS hot in the streets of Milan. She walked cautiously down the front steps of the Palazzo in her stiletto heels. They were one of the things she'd been glad to leave behind in Italy. But now? They might just prove useful. Once she'd got the hang of them again.

Rose carefully negotiated the cobbled street that led to her destination. It was the only place Giovanni ever went. Portofino. A complex of intimate dining rooms, bars and lounges, it met every mood of its wealthy patrons.

"Signora Visconti! How lovely to see you again. I'd heard that you were back."

Could Rose hear a certain panic in the maitre d's voice or was she getting paranoid?

"A table for one please—in your main bar."

"Si, Signora. Come this way. We are always pleased to accommodate you."

True to his word, the maitre d' found a table in the busy bar and Rose let him seat her before she looked around. No sign of Giovanni yet. But he'd be here. The maitre d' would make sure of that. Wherever Giovanni was, he'd be informed of her presence here within the hour.

. . .

Two hours later she was the centre of attention. She didn't kid herself that it was her sparkling conversation or any deep connection she was making with the half-a-dozen men vying for her smile. She wriggled uncomfortably in the slim-fitting dress that she'd bought in a fit of pique three years ago and had never worn. Like all the rest of her clothes she'd left behind, it had remained in the wardrobe, as if Giovanni had always expected her to return. She'd never worn this particular dress. It had been too revealing, Giovanni had claimed, and so she'd gone along with his wishes and it had remained unworn. But tonight it was having the exact effect she'd planned—except with the wrong men. Where was he? She tugged the dress down over her thighs, crossed her legs and sipped yet more wine for courage.

Her glass was immediately refilled. She wondered, briefly, how many glasses she'd had before the thought evaporated hazily at the sensation of her straight and silky hair tickling the heated skin of her bare shoulders and back.

"You have beautiful hair, bella." One of the young men—younger than her, she estimated—emboldened perhaps by her unfocussed gaze, leaned forward and ran his hands through it before tickling her breast with a lock that had begun to curl in the heat.

That focused her sharply. "Enough," she batted away his hand and stood up, ignoring the urgings from her companions to remain. Either Giovanni hadn't heard about her presence in the notorious bar, or he didn't care. If he'd cared, he would have been there fighting the men off. Time to go.

She rose and felt the room move. She must have drunk more wine than she'd thought. She walked unsteadily out to the balcony, followed by a couple of the men. Suddenly the cool English tones of Giovanni's assistant, Simon, rang out.

"Signora Rose, allow me."

She'd never been so pleased to see anybody in her life. She took his arm and left the building.

"Am I glad to see you Simon."

"So it would seem Signora Rose."

He held her firmly as they walked the block back to the palazzo.

"Do you often go there, Simon?"

"Rarely. But it was suggested that you might need some assistance tonight. I'd been there a while before I thought it timely to make my move."

"Who did the suggesting?"

"Signore Visconti of course. He wanted to make sure you arrived home safely."

She stopped in astonishment and stood unsteadily. "How did he know I was there?"

"I think it would be more fitting for him to tell you that. But he was aware of your, er, evening out, but—"

"But didn't want to do anything about it himself. Thought he'd get you to do the dirty work."

"Now, Signora Rose. Firstly we should move. You'll get us both run over standing in the middle of the road like this. And secondly escorting you from the club was hardly dirty work."

"Hmm!" Rose began walking once more, her shoes stabbing the cobbled stones with irritation. He'd been there, or had known she was, and had deliberately sent one of his employees to sort her out. Just like an errant child who needed to be watched over by an impartial carer. Damn it! He hadn't even cared enough to make sure she was all right himself!

She could feel the tears begin. She really must have drunk more wine than she'd thought. Those guys must have been topping up her glass without her noticing.

So that's all she was to him. Someone to be organized,

cared for from a distance, just like one of his employees. She'd tried to find him, to spend time with him, but instead she'd found interest from the wrong men and even Giovanni's jealousy had failed to respond. It was stupid: jealousy didn't equal love. She knew that. But it was his total lack of response that got to her. It could only mean one thing. He didn't love her any more.

"Please don't cry." Simon's voice held an edge of panic.

"I'm not crying."

She continued not to cry all the way back to the Palazzo where she used Simon's scarf to wipe away the mascara rings before entering. He opened the door for her.

"Good night, signora, I'll leave you now."

"Night." Once inside she fell back against the closed door and listened to his muffled steps retreat to his nearby apartment. None of the staff lived in the house. She was quite alone. Except for Giovanni, somewhere in the depths of the house.

She breathed in the polished dark emptiness of the grand hall. The clock clanged two chimes, for once in time. He'd be in bed by now. She slipped off her shoes and began to walk down the hall. Head down, watching her step, intent on getting to her bedroom unnoticed.

Suddenly the top of her head bumped into something. She screamed and jumped back.

"Walking around without looking where you're going; is that a New Zealand habit that you've acquired?"

"Where the hell did you come from?"

"I've been waiting for you. Come in here."

She followed him into his study, desperately trying to keep the waves of nausea at bay and clear her head. She sat down in the soft suede chair and realized that there was little chance of recovering sufficiently to win a game of wits with him. But she'd give it her best shot.

"What do you want Giovanni? To tell me off for having fun?"

"Did you?"

"What? Have fun? Of course. How could I not? Good wine and good company. *Very* good company."

She watched carefully, noticing a tightening around his jaw. "You certainly appear to have had a surfeit of both."

"How would you know? You sent Simon to watch over me."

He glanced quickly at her before pouring himself a drink and sitting down at his desk. She watched him suspiciously.

"You were there, weren't you?"

"Of course. I was told that you were dining there and thought I would join you. But even after half an hour you'd acquired quite a gathering around your table."

"So you left?"

"No. I watched and waited. But got bored watching your awkward flirtations and decided to leave the job to Simon. Whatever your reason for such behavior, I thought it best if I weren't there to witness it."

"Didn't like seeing your wife with other men?"

"Didn't like seeing my employee make a fool of herself." Giovanni snapped back. "Don't do it again Rose. You are hopelessly inept and besides, your obvious intention has failed. You have not made me jealous."

Giovanni sat back and watched as she swayed slightly in her chair, about to deny his charge but then, for whatever reason, changing her mind.

He'd like to wring the neck of each one of the young men who had devoured Rose with their eyes. He'd seen what they'd seen and he'd imagined what each one of them had imagined. They were new to the establishment otherwise they wouldn't have dared to try to ensnare his wife from under his nose.

But for all the lusting after her body, and for all the jealousy of watching other men covet what should be his, it was his overwhelming sense of tenderness he felt for her that shocked him.

When she'd looked uneasy at some remark he'd wanted to kiss away the frown on her forehead; when she'd flicked away her hair from her breasts that one of the bastards had lain there, he'd wanted to smooth it away and kiss the place where it had touched; when she'd finally risen to go, he'd wanted to wrap her in his arms and carry her away to safety.

For he had been there and watched her performance from the manager's office where he couldn't be seen and where enough money had secured the manager's silence.

He cared for her all right, but he'd learned his lesson two years ago: one, that his overpowering jealousy had killed their relationship and two, if he revealed the depths of his love for her, she would only run away once more. She'd been born a free spirit and her unbalanced mother had turned her into an independent one by necessity. It had been his fault—all of it. But he'd given her time, he tried to show her that his jealousy was under control but even his new-found control had limits. And he'd just reached them. He was still determined to keep his distance emotionally, but he sure as hell was going to keep close to her physically. There was going to be no repeat of tonight.

≈

IMPOSSIBLE.

It was the only word she could think of to describe the past few weeks. They'd been together—Giovanni had made sure she was always close by—but separate. It was as if a massive, invisible wall had grown between them overnight. They'd been overly polite to each other. Going out of their way not to touch, or to brush past. At least she'd made progress on her work.

Alberto was as guilty as sin. All she had to do was prove it. And it wouldn't take too much longer. So absorbed was she that Rose didn't hear Simon enter until he coughed politely.

"Signora Rose, Signore Visconti has requested that you leave your work for today and join him."

Rose frowned and continued to scroll through sheets of company accounts. "Thank you Simon. However, I can imagine that Signore Visconti used different words and that you've kindly translated it into polite English."

He pursed his lips ruefully. The twinkle in his eyes said it all.

"Tell Signore that I'm not hungry and that I've work to do."

Simon raised his eyebrow, questioning the wisdom of her reply.

She looked up at him. "I know, I know. But I can't get away, I'm on to something here."

"Of course. I will relay your message to Signore Visconti." He inclined his head respectfully and closed the door quietly behind him.

And besides, she muttered under her breath, she couldn't take spending every minute of her down time with a man whose clothes she wanted to rip off and who was patently not interested in her. He wanted business; he would have business. Being so close to him while he was so constantly cool with her, was driving her insane.

If he only wanted her to work, then why the hell was he intent on dominating her entire life?

Wherever she went, he was there.

The past few weeks had been murder. He'd insisted on cozy little lunch catch-ups; on formal dinners and now he was insisting on her attending a high-society charity party. He was treating her with all the respect and distance of a work colleague: nothing more, nothing less. But making sure she attended every social event on his calendar. Well she damn well wasn't going to be treated like a work colleague. She was his wife and lover. Former lover, she amended.

The door swung open sharply making her jump. She knew who it was but refused to turn around.

"Get changed and then meet me in the drawing room."

"I'm busy."

"It was not a request."

"Hey, I'm on to something and the sooner I get it tied up, the sooner I can go. That's what you want, isn't it?"

"What have you found?"

She noticed that he hadn't answered her question.

"Some discrepancies unaccounted for."

"There are always discrepancies."

"Not as big and not as regular as these. Besides the same name keeps popping up."

"Alberto."

She looked up at him suddenly. "You knew all along didn't you?"

"I suspected."

"Well, it looks as though your suspicions are correct." She narrowed her gaze. "Anyway, why did you need me? You could have simply dealt with Alberto yourself."

"I need proof. Suspicions aren't sufficient. My brother and I are not close, as you know. My mother would simply refuse to believe any allegations I make without evidence."

She turned away from Giovanni and pressed her eyes tight shut. She knew well. The two were opposites with a pile of emotional issues thrown into the mix for good measure. Their relationship had always been a minefield ready to explode. She'd made sure that she wasn't the touch paper two years ago. But it looked as though Giovanni wanted her to provide the match now.

"I can't give you the proof yet. But I'm close." She swung around to face him. "Giovanni. Are you sure you want to do this? The amounts involved are nothing compared to the company's turnover. You're going to blow the family apart."

"The family was blown apart many years ago by my mother's infidelities and my father's violence. And my brother has wasted his life."

"And continues to do so at some resort or other."

And boy, was she relieved. She didn't know where he was and she didn't want to know. So long as he was nowhere near her and not expected any time soon, that was good enough for her.

"You miss him?" Giovanni's voice was a whisper.

She looked at him in disbelief. "No, of course not. Why do you ask?"

"I received the distinct impression that you like him. A lot."

She shook her head. "I don't know where you got that idea from—probably Alberto." She raised her eyebrows. "The concept of a woman not attracted to Alberto is foreign to him."

It was as if she'd struck a match, lit a light in his eyes. For the first time in the weeks since she'd returned, Rose saw the old familiar spark of heat, of passion, of humor once more in his eyes. It warmed her like nothing else, attracting her to its flame.

She rose and stepped closer.

"Your family has a lot to answer for Giovanni." More than he would ever know. "But it's your father you blame most, isn't it?"

"What he did tore our family apart. Tore me apart," he added softly. "And made my mother's philandering even worse. Without his violence she would have been less unhappy."

"And spent more time with you and your brother. Loved you more."

"She loved my brother enough. For myself, it isn't important. No, it was my father's weakness that I despise. My mother," he shrugged, "she knew no better."

Rose's eyes shot open. "Your mother never gave you what you needed most. She abandoned you." She touched his arm.

He looked down at her hand in dull puzzlement.

"As did you, Rose."

She snatched back her hand as if he'd scalded her.

"I had no choice, Giovanni. You don't understand."

"If you'd tried to explain, I may have understood. You obviously didn't believe I would and you could have been right. But the time for explanations is gone—I'm no longer interested in them."

"Then why am I here?" she blazed. "Why drag me across the other side of the world where I was happy."

"You weren't happy. You *existed* merely."

"How would you know?"

"Because I *know* you—with or without explanations, with or without logic—I *know* you. I know you on a level that you will never understand."

"Know me perhaps, but want me no longer."

"Why do you think I do not want you?"

He moved closer to her, his head tilted to one side, his expression curious. She stood tall, trying to hold her own under his scrutiny.

"Because apart from that night on the plane you haven't touched me."

"And you would welcome my touch?"

His hands were firmly pushed into the pockets of his

trousers but he stepped closer to her again until she could sense the comfort of his body so close.

"I, I didn't say that."

"But you implied it."

She shook her head as if to shake herself out of the hole that she'd just created. She tried to step around him but he was too quick and blocked her way.

"Answer my question."

"I don't intend to. A minute ago you wanted me to get ready for a charity ball. Well, let me go and get dressed."

"No." He lazily drew a hand from his pocket and let one finger drift down her cheek and around her chin, holding it there briefly before tilting it up so that she had no choice but to look him in the eye. "Not yet. You want me to touch you, well I am touching you. How does that make you feel?"

There was no way in this world she was about to tell him of the electrical storm his touch ignited in her body.

She shrugged in what she hoped was a nonchalant way. "OK I suppose."

His beautiful lips quirked briefly into a smile.

"OK? I will have to work on that, obviously."

"Don't worry about it." She tried to shake her head free.

"But I do."

"You haven't up to now. We've been together for three weeks now and nothing—no sign of interest. What's changed?"

"Simple *cara*. You've just answered my second question."

He dropped his hand from her face, smiled at her obvious confusion and walked away.

"What question? What was it?"

"Don't be late. We're leaving in one hour."

He didn't even bother to turn around.

She followed him out of the room and watched him retreat to his suite of rooms.

CHAPTER 6

*I*t was still possible.

It was all she could think as, in a daze, she walked to her room and flicked on the shower and undressed automatically. As she stepped out of her clothes, a cool evening breeze, fresh from the mountains, blew through the open window and a blast of air hit her skin, sensitizing her body.

It was still possible that he wanted her.

Whatever question she'd inadvertently answered had triggered a response she'd feared was dead.

As she stepped into the shower, the harsh spray of water stung her body and the kaleidoscope of her memories collapsed, flashing one after another, forming a new image.

His no holds barred passion during their brief marriage together; his choice of words when he found her again in New Zealand—"you are mine still"—after he kissed her; and his constant presence over the previous few weeks.

They added up to a picture of someone whose formidable pride had forced him to bury his feelings for her deep, but not so deep that she couldn't unearth them again.

She had to leave in a few weeks anyway, before Alberto returned. She needed Giovanni to know what she felt for him, she wanted to experience his love before she left. Besides there was always the possibility that Alberto might disappear, might simply go away—seduced by a young brunette, or an older one—go far away, where Giovanni's rage at what Alberto had done to Rose wouldn't have the fatal consequences she feared.

If he still wanted her—even a little—there was still hope. And hope was a potent thing: it extended boundaries, knocked down walls, protected and nurtured the tiniest of seeds.

As if reinforcing the power of her emotional shift she was slammed back physically into her life by the sensory force of the shower, registering each touch, sight, smell with abnormal vividness. Hope blossomed further in this sensory overdrive where sensation layered upon sensation, awaking memories of Giovanni touching her, making love to her.

Hope and sensation—it was a heady mix.

She felt the steamy velvetiness of the glass doors, soaked in steam, upon her palms and breathed in deeply the scents from the cosmetics on the shelf and from the flowers that filled the window box on her balcony, letting the power of the water blast away the shadows that haunted her. Shadows that had to be forced into the light. Because only there would they do no harm.

She had to tell Giovanni the truth. Had to tell him everything.

She lathered her hands and ran them down the length of her body, relishing the feel of her skin under the silky soap. She closed her eyes and saw Giovanni, his eyes, looking into hers as he explored her body. Heat shimmered deep inside her.

She turned the shower to cold and let the fierce shock

slam into her gnawing need for him. She had to have him once more.

She smiled as her thoughts took shape.

AFTER APPLYING HER LIPSTICK, Rose stood back from the mirror, knowing what she would see because she knew what she was feeling. But it was still a shock.

Gone was the cool, controlled businesswoman and gone was the recluse she'd become in New Zealand. The tension between the two images was resolved in the sophisticated and sensual woman who looked back at her from the mirror.

Her hair, for once, was untouched by the straightening iron. It fell around her shoulders, framing her face in abandon of wild curls, tickling her bare back and skimming her breasts, keeping them in a state of acute awareness.

The vintage grey sheath of a dress fell in drapes over her body—sheer, leaving nothing to the imagination. It was amongst the wardrobe of clothes he'd bought for her all those years ago. It was a blatantly sexual dress and that's what she wanted now.

She wore no underwear to spoil the line. The deep V at the front, the shoestring straps, the plunging back, combined with the skim of satin over her skin to send a clear message.

She would never have worn such a dress before Giovanni —or even during their marriage. She'd always dressed very properly, from instinct and from concern that she'd arouse his jealousy. But that was before she'd lost him. And now she'd found him again and she wanted him to see what she'd become: what he'd made her.

She wanted him as she'd never wanted a man before. She was no virgin besotted with her man as she had been three years before. She was a grown woman who'd experienced the joy of giving and receiving love and the pain of denying love

—both to herself and her lover. She was not the same girl Giovanni had married. And she intended to show him the difference tonight.

GIOVANNI STEPPED into the waiting limo after her and leaned over to whisper in her ear.

"Why are you wearing that dress?"

Rose looked down at the dress that revealed so much.

"This dress?" She smoothed a non-existent wrinkle over her thighs.

"*That* dress."

"You don't like it?"

"I think I might not like the reason you're wearing it."

"You didn't answer my question."

"You didn't answer mine. Why are you wearing that dress?"

She shrugged. "It just felt, appropriate, somehow."

"Appropriate?" his eyes narrowed under dark brows. "It's a wonder you can breathe in it."

She sat upright and pushed her chest out lightly as she took a deep breath. "Difficult, but not impossible."

She noticed his eyes drop and fix on her breasts, their curves exposed by the plunging neckline.

It was not going to be so hard—to seduce her husband.

He raised his eyes to meet hers, narrowed and assessing.

"And your hair. You have it loose, like a schoolgirl. Like in bed. Why?"

She shivered the hair around her shoulders, enjoying the tickle of it on her bare back.

"Haven't I been working hard?"

He nodded.

"Am I not allowed to let my hair down sometimes? And my dress," she smoothed her hand across the silk that clung to her body like a second skin, taking a deep feminine satis-faction in the way his eyes followed her hand. "After all you did buy it for me."

He shrugged his shoulders. "A long time ago."

"It's beautiful, isn't it?"

"There is little to it. I can't believe the price they charged me for it."

"Ha! So you do remember it."

"Vaguely. You needed some evening wear and I thought—"

A blaze of lights illuminated the inside of the limo and Rose could see his gaze fixed upon her eyes.

"Thought?"

"That the color would suit you."

"Like the grey northern skies?"

"No." He twisted a strand of her hair between his fingers. Her heart thumped uncomfortably in her chest. "Like the warm grey of violet as the sun sinks beyond the horizon, just before night falls."

"Seductive talk." She took a deep breath.

"That is what you are wanting, no?"

"And why would I want that? You made it plain you weren't interested."

"Perhaps you wish to show me your strength, take revenge on me at some level, for bringing you to Italy." He took her hand, weaving his fingers between hers, holding it between their bodies. "But you are not like that. You are strong with no need to prove anything. You were never competitive."

She raised her eyebrows. "So insightful. There is only room for one competitor in a relationship. And you have enough of those genes for both of us."

"And what relationship is that, Rose? Because I do not believe we have one any more."

His words hit hard but she tried to suppress the flicker of panic. He knew she wanted him but she didn't want to give him the satisfaction of knowing how much.

"You are so right, Giovanni. A marriage does not a relationship make. What constitutes a relationship in your book?"

"To begin with, an attraction: a lust, a physical wanting."

She felt a frisson of that same lust stir in her gut. "Umm."

The limo pulled up outside the venue.

He jumped out and opened her door for her.

She lifted her dress away from her stilettos and stepped out carefully beside him, into the marble entrance.

She could feel the soft fabric of the dress rub lightly against her body, teasing her as much as him.

"The kind of attraction that kicks in when the other is close," he continued. "When the other person is not even touching."

"What kind is that?" She wanted him to elaborate. "So much attraction takes place in the imagination." And she needed to know what was in his imagination right now.

He laughed. "If one's love affairs only took place in one's imagination then life would be a lot easier. Come." He took her arm in his.

"So that's lust dealt with. But that can't be all that constitutes a relationship. Anything else?"

He tracked his finger up her arm, leaving a trail of goose bumps. "Respect."

She leaned into his neck and breathed. "Ahh! Such a good old-fashioned virtue."

The porter ushered them inside the grand hotel.

"I'd forgotten what a beautiful building this is. Milan has so many hidden treasures I've heard about and not seen."

"Then we must remedy that. But not tonight."

Instead of going directly into the ballroom, Giovanni pulled her to one side and into a small ante room.

"A detour?"

"Si. A little practical work around respect." He pulled her close and ran his hands down her sides, caressing her thighs over the silky fabric. "I cherish traditional values. My respect for your legs and your breasts," he ran a finger over the top of her nipple that was visible from beneath the sheer fabric, "knows no bounds."

She tipped her neck back, reveling in the feel of her long hair tumbling around her shoulders, and the heat of his breath against her breasts. "Then I shall kiss you chastely, as a symbol of my respect for your respect."

She pressed her hands to his chest and raised her closed lips to his, aware of the pounding of his heart beneath her hand and the brief opening of his mouth as her lips left his. He wanted more. She smiled. Who was in control now?

It was all she could do not press her lips back to his and take what he so obviously wanted. But it was important that she keep the upper hand. She wanted to move Giovanni, make him forget his cool, remind him of what they once had. And she could only do that if she was in control.

She nipped lightly at his ear lobe before breathing into his neck and kissing his glorious olive skin. Her heart thudded in her chest as his scent infiltrated her senses and, deep within, her body readied itself for him. Like it or not, her body recognized her mate from his scent alone. She drew back. She'd always had a thing for his skin. She drew in a ragged breath and ran her fingers up into his hair until her hands enclosed his face. She tried to stop them shaking as she looked into his eyes, deep and dark and dangerous as the night. Waiting to see if her prey would bite.

"You're playing with fire, *cara*."

"Perhaps I feel cold?"

She moved slightly against his hips, until she felt him firm against her. She watched his mouth tighten further, still intent on restraint, whatever his body might desire.

She pulled away again, enjoying the feeling of control as he instinctively moved to pull her back to him. "Is that it? Desire and respect. Is that all you need in a relationship?"

He grabbed a handful of her hair and pulled her to him, their foreheads pressed one against the other. "It must be a meeting of minds also."

She closed her eyes as their lips met briefly. "Umm, minds can be so under-estimated," she muttered before pulling back in mock innocence, dredging up her last remaining shred of self control. "You'd be surprised what mine is thinking right now."

His mouth was firm, only his eyes revealed his desire. "Nothing surprises me about you. You are the sort of woman who can do anything she sets her mind to. Intelligent, strong-minded, uncompromising. And mercurial. Here one minute and gone the next."

"I'm here now." All pretense forgotten she pressed her lips to his and urged them to open, to allow her tongue entrance. She wanted everything he could give. She wanted to lose the control she'd been enjoying only moments earlier.

He responded with a savagery that she met pace for pace. His mouth devoured hers, seeking the release that echoed her own needs. His tongue twisted around hers, probing, exploring her heat. Her breathing quickened and her mind numbed as passion overtook her.

He cupped her bottom under his hands and lifted her to him, pressing her intimately as he turned around and pushed her back onto a table, pressing her legs open with his leg, her hips held tight between his hips and his hands. Her dress wrinkled up her thighs as her legs were pushed open. Her hands came around his back and pushed under his shirt, desperate for the feel of his skin against her hands. But instead of satisfying her needs, it inflamed them further.

She pulled his head to hers, as she lay down on the table. She closed her eyes as his tongue explored firstly her mouth, then her neck, and then her breasts. She moaned as his touch roused her body to a state of desire she couldn't remember ever having felt.

"Tell me," he ordered quietly. "Tell me what you're feeling."

"I want you."

He licked her lazily again. "How much?"

"You can feel how much."

"And I can see." He stood back, holding her firmly. "You are beautiful." His voice was thick with desire. He drew close to her once more and picked her up, pressing her to him with his hands around her bottom. He kissed her again. It was a kiss of ownership but she had no grounds for objection.

Suddenly, there was a sharp rap at the door.

"Signore Visconti? It's nearly time." It was Simon, obviously keeping a closer eye on Giovanni than he'd anticipated.

"Cazzarola!"

"Ignore him."

"I can't. I'm giving the introduction. I'll have to go."

He let her dress fall before dropping a chaste kiss on her forehead. "Remember this moment. We will continue later."

"Don't worry. I won't forget."

THEY SLIPPED in amongst the glittering crowds of moneyed elite.

Milan was the capital of Italian business, media and fashion and it was fully evident tonight. The wealthy socialites and business leaders were out in their finery. The old castle, now converted to a hotel was glorious with its gothic architecture that had miraculously survived centuries of war. The large reception room was filled with the sound of chamber music, laughter, clinking glasses and the buzz of casual chatter. The Milanese had perfected the art of the cocktail hour until it had become the cocktail evening. The drinks flowed and so did the Lombard delicacies.

Giovanni was immediately beckoned over to the group of organizers.

Rose slipped into a seat at a table unannounced, introducing herself by habit by her maiden name. She was used to people looking her up and down and assessing her. Without a known name she was accepted on her looks but basically ignored, which was fine with her.

She listened idly to the chatter of the ladies about the fashion industry as her own mind wandered, inevitably, to Giovanni. She watched him as he talked with a group of men at the side of the stage. Everyone paled into insignificance beside him. Not just because of his stunning looks or his confident use of his power, but because of his complete lack of self consciousness. His clothes were of the best but, once dressed, he was oblivious to them. His eyes didn't scan the room restlessly; he had a depth of intelligence and perception that didn't allow that. The whole package made him compelling. She fingered her recently kissed lips, remembering and imagining the night ahead.

She hoped Giovannni's part in the evening would be over soon and they could escape, back to the Palazzo, back to the ante room. Wherever they could be alone.

She sighed and sat back.

"You seem to be in a world of your own."

She smiled at her neighbor. "Yes, a little. It's a while since I've been in Milan. A few years and I feel like a stranger."

"Well you've chosen a good party for a debut. Everyone is

here. Giovanni has made it the charity of the moment. But really, who'd have thought it? Scholarships for the poor. It's hardly a sexy charity to support is it?"

Sexy it might not be, but it was Rose's own charity; a charity that, when they had been together, Giovanni had scarcely seemed to notice.

She smiled.

"I'm sure the recipients find it pretty sexy."

Her neighbor leaned forwarded confidentially. "If you've been out of circulation for a while then you need an urgent gossip session."

"No, really," Rose laughed, watching Giovanni approach the microphone.

Her neighbor followed her gaze.

"We can start with his family if you like."

"What?" distracted Rose could hardly think what the woman was talking about.

"You'd think the Viscontis had everything: money, power, looks. The scandal around Giovanni's wife leaving him for Alberto was quite something but Alberto's gone and topped it now."

"What?" Rose whispered, feeing the blood drain from her face. She shifted to face the woman. "What?" she practically shouted.

"His wife left him—had enough of his jealous ways— rumor has it that he was violent towards her."

Rose shook with anger.

"That's nonsense. Rumor-mongering rubbish."

"Pretty spot on I should say. My sources are close to the family."

But before Rose could retort she was hushed by the people around her as Giovanni began his speech, commanding the audience, engaging everyone by his presence and words. Words that, she assumed, were as convincing as usual. She heard not a thing. All Rose could do was watch and imagine Giovanni suffering as he heard the rumors and tried not to believe them.

Everyone believed that she'd left Giovanni for Alberto? Why would she? Why would anyone in their right mind prefer the dilettante Alberto to Giovanni?

Alberto's attack had killed her unborn child and killed a part of herself. He'd damn nearly raped her—would have if she hadn't used all she'd learned from the self defense classes she'd taken as a young woman. She'd taken any kind of free classes to get herself out of the life her mother led. At least that class had proved useful.

Alberto must have circulated the rumor. But it wasn't what the world believed that hurt her to the quick. Giovanni must have believed it. After all she hadn't been around to deny it.

As soon as the applause faded Rose leaned over once more to her informant.

"Giovanni Visconti, violent? Never. Surely you mean Alberto?"

"Well," the woman raised her eyebrows in delight at a receptive audience. "Alberto is another story. The new scandal about his rape—oops, sorry—his *alleged* rape of a young woman will be hard for the family to live down. He's not allowed to leave Switzerland until the trial is over."

Jesus.

Rose slumped in her chair. The rush of talk and applause conflated into one loud roar, filling her ears and her body with panic and sickness.

Alberto on trial for rape.

She'd persuaded herself that his attack on her was a one off: a culmination of the enmity that existed between the brothers. If she'd supposed for one minute that he would attack another woman, let alone rape a woman, she would have spoken up. But she'd let her own private fears dominate her world and she'd fled, saying nothing.

And a woman had suffered because of it.

She felt devastated, remembering the pain—both physical and mental—that she'd suffered. And she'd allowed another woman to suffer the same fate.

But it was too late now. It was his word against hers and it was two years ago. All the evidence had vanished. There was nothing she could do for the woman. Nothing she could do for Giovanni.

She shivered and pulled her wrap around her shoulders.

"My dear. I hardly believe you've heard a word I've been saying. Tired of gossip already?"

"Pardon? I'm sorry," she looked around, suddenly claustrophobic. "I have to go."

"But the party has only just begun."

"It's over for me."

She scraped the chair back on the marble floor and stumbled out, barely aware that Giovanni had disappeared from the stage.

The night had turned cool, but still humidity hung heavy in the air. Storm weather she thought absently and walked out across the square, in the general direction of the palazzo.

The Duomo, floodlit and majestic reared up before her, a symbol of the might of the great Milanese families—Visconti, Sforzo. There were exceptions to greatness in every family. Pity was that Giovanni should be tainted by the same brush as his brother. The thought of his innocence beside the blood on Alberto's hands sickened her further.

What had she done by running away? Given Alberto free rein to indulge his sick fantasies, that's what.

Her head gripped with the pain of unshed tears; it rent her body and found no release. She stumbled in her stilettos on the uneven paving and clung briefly to a railing to recover herself.

A wolf whistle rent the air. "Drunk too much, girlie?"

The man spoke English with a heavy unidentifiable accent. She looked up to see that he was part of a group of men, beer bottles in hand, who was watching her, assessingly.

She shook her head. Still numb by her recent discovery, she felt no threat or danger from the group. What pain could anyone inflict on her now that she hadn't already experienced? She deserved it anyway.

"No. I'm fine." She made to step forward but found her way blocked. "I said I'm fine."

"I don't think you are. I think you need some help."

"And I think you should listen to the lady and walk away while you still can."

She closed her eyes tightly at the sound of Giovanni's voice, waiting for his explosion. None came. When she opened them again the men had disappeared leaving only Giovanni.

"Did they touch you?" His voice was tight.

She shook her head. "No. It's my fault."

"What is your fault exactly?"

How could she explain to him that everything was. She'd made one bad decision after another, leaving other people to pick up the pieces. Well, no more.

"Being here—alone. Being here too late."

"You're talking in riddles. Tell me. Something happened in there. What did you hear?"

How could she tell him? He'd despise her for her weakness, for her guilt. She couldn't bear it.

"You won't tell me?"

She shook her head.

"Again. You hide things from me. Come, I'll get Simon to take you home."

A brief phone call had Simon draw up within minutes.

Giovanni put his arm around her and drew her to him, helping her across the road to the limousine. She yielded to his strength, finding brief and superficial comfort from him. But she stood alone on this. Her guilt was her own. There was nothing anyone could do to help.

He drew her face to his. "Still nothing to say to me?"

She searched his face, seeing the signs of the past few years evident in the etched lines of his face, and, most of all in the expression in his eyes—deeper now, more knowing, more aware. She'd done that to him. She'd done enough.

She shook her head once more.

He opened the door for her. "We spoke of what made a relationship. Well, *cara*, there is one more thing a relationship needs to make it work; one thing that you will not give me. Perhaps I do not deserve it, I don't know. But you need to look more closely. As I said, things change, people change. Perhaps I've changed. Perhaps you cannot give me the one thing we do not have."

She felt dazed, unable to comprehend his meaning.

"And what is that?"

"Trust. And without that, we have nothing."

He slammed the door firmly shut and the car pulled off leaving him standing, watching her disappear into the night.

GIOVANNI WALKED BACK to the party. His presence was required. He hesitated on the steps and turned momentarily, watching the limo disappear around the corner.

His body ached with need.

He hadn't anticipated that she'd turn the tables on him

and try to seduce him. And he'd fallen for it. Until she'd had second thoughts.

The fact that she ran away, rather than trust him with the truth hurt more than anything. He was the person whom everyone relied on to fix things up and he couldn't help his own wife. She had to know, but no amount of telling would convince her. She had to see that he had changed, that he could be trusted.

In the meantime, he had some uncomfortable nights— and days—ahead of him.

He entered the baroque lobby—all wedding-cake plaster and gilt moldings—and watched as Milan's elite glittered and sparkled before him.

None of it could touch him like she could.

She was his match in every way.

She thought she was turning up the heat on him. Testing him, seeing how he would respond. Well, if little girls liked to play with fire then he'd give her some.

And this time, she wouldn't be able to back out so easily. She needed to be pushed outside her comfort zone, shaken up a bit: made to realize what he already knew.

CHAPTER 7

She'd never trusted anyone. How could she start now?

Mechanically she slipped out of the dress that had symbolized new hope only hours before, and pulled on her robe, dragging the knot too tightly across her waist.

How dare anyone reproach her for not trusting? What could anybody, least of all Giovanni, know about her upbringing?

She walked across to the rear window that overlooked the inner courtyard, and opened it up wide to the storm. Darkness lay all around. No sign of life, except the wild weather. No light from Giovanni's suite opposite. No doubt he was still at the party, taking up with some woman where they'd left off. The thought made her feel sick. She left the window open, despite the rain that slanted in through the window, splattering large, dark drops onto the pale wooden floor. On a clear day she could see the icy peaks of the Alps in the distance. But tonight there was nothing to see: no external sign of an existence beyond herself. There was only her in this little pocket of loneliness.

She might have been a teenager again, living her life and dreams in the box room of the Council flat: using her paper-round money for her lunches, hiding the rent money in a jar in her room, screwing a lock on her door for those nights when her mother was entertaining. At fourteen she knew the only person who could look after her—give her a future—was herself.

How could Giovanni not understand that trusting people hadn't been an option growing up, not if she'd wanted to climb out of the hole that was her mother's life? It had been the only thing that had got her through all of that. And more.

Marriage and children hadn't been on her radar but somehow Giovanni had slipped under it and into her heart.

But she'd insisted she kept working, insisted that she maintain her independence financially and she'd tried her hardest to maintain an emotional independence. She'd built her whole life around it.

Only trusting herself. The only person she could be sure of.

She unclipped her necklace and lay it in the box, alongside the other jewelry Giovanni had bought her. It was all of the best taste—unusual vintage pieces mostly—he knew what she liked. He knew her well.

She grimaced and closed the box.

He was right, she didn't trust him with the truth. But how could she if he could believe Alberto's lies? If he could believe them, then why would he believe her story—a version of events that seemed even more improbable than Alberto's? Sad thing was, they actually happened.

She turned away from the box of memories and went over to the bathroom. She flicked on the light and saw her reflection in the mirror opposite: pale, pensive and confused. She flicked off the light quickly.

She paced across to the window once more but turned

quickly, forcing herself to remember the events of that night. They came in flashes, some scenes felt more viscerally, rather than remembered, others imprinted in every visual detail on her brain.

That evening, two years ago, Giovanni had been due home. They'd been separated for six months with only fleeting reunions in New York in the early months. She'd been feeling stifled in Milan by Giovanni's jealousy and had accepted a contract in Hong Kong. She'd needed to get away for a while. Discovering she was pregnant made her feelings of being trapped worse but it took only a few months for her to know her future was with him. But not immediately. They both had to work out their contracts.

It had been an important, delicate deal for Giovanni, one that he had to oversee personally while Rose completed her work in Hong Kong. She knew if Giovanni had discovered she was pregnant, he would have insisted on staying with her and the deal would have failed. And, along with it, the future of those who depended on them. She couldn't have that on her conscience.

And besides, it was only to have been for a few months.

At first it had been simple. She'd managed to hide her pregnancy easily. After all she'd hardly put on any weight and had remained fit. But then the passing of the months seemed to slow. She'd had to make excuses not to see him. She knew he hadn't understood why they couldn't meet. It had nearly killed her, but she'd believed the pain of separation would pale into insignificance once they were together again. A new life would begin for them then.

At last, after six long months Giovanni had been due to return. She'd flown in earlier that day and had been about to go directly to Lugano, where they'd planned their reunion, when Alberto had called, informing her that Giovanni's plane was arriving early and that he would meet her at the Palazzo.

Giovanni's supposed change of plan should have raised her suspicions but she'd been so excited that nothing could have clouded her happiness. She'd laughed to herself. So like Giovanni. After months apart he couldn't wait another half hour.

She'd arrived at the Palazzo early. Everything had been ready: the staff dismissed, the mood intimate, everything just as he liked it. And then she waited. But not for long.

She hadn't been entirely surprised when Alberto had shown up. She'd thought it must have had something to do with business. And then, when he'd taken her to Giovanni's suite of rooms, his bedroom, she'd been scared—convinced that Giovanni had fallen ill.

But there had been no Giovanni.

Instead there had been only a clumsy attempt at seduction. She'd even misconstrued *that* at the beginning, not taking him seriously. But if there was one thing that angered Alberto, it was being laughed at.

He was not a large man, but Rose had soon found out that a wiry strength lay in those arms. A simple pass turned into a sexual attack that Rose had been unable to halt.

The weakness that she'd always seen in Alberto had been masking a lethal mix of frustration and anger at his lack of power that manifested itself in a display of perversion and violence of which Rose had not thought him capable.

She'd not fought back at first. It was something that had haunted her afterwards. But she couldn't. Primitive feelings of protection of her unborn child had made her try to diffuse the situation and not retaliate. But as the situation had deteriorated she'd been forced to defend herself.

But it had been too late.

Bleeding, she'd driven back to Milan, to the hospital and seen the best doctors in an effort to save her baby. But it wasn't to be.

She'd stayed at a hotel only long enough to bury her baby before buying a ticket to the farthest destination she could think of—New Zealand.

She'd acted purely on instinct, grieving for the loss of her baby and terrified about what Giovanni would do when he discovered what had happened. Giovanni's childhood had been dominated by his father's uncontrollable rages—something he feared that he, himself, had inherited. He'd always hated his brother and Rose knew that this one act would literally make him see red and nothing else: his passions would overtake him and he would hit Alberto and she didn't know if he'd be able to stop.

So she did what she always did, trusted no-one with the truth and moved on. Giovanni would get over her. She'd soon just be another brunette to chalk down to experience. One, presumably, he'd rather forget.

What she hadn't expected was for Alberto to fabricate the story that she'd been trying to seduce him. He'd claimed she'd finally become desperate at the thought of being with Giovanni again and had invited Alberto to call on her the night before Giovanni was due home.

Did she do the wrong thing? Should she have trusted Giovanni with what happened? Possibly. She still didn't know. But she'd been grieving for the loss of her child. And her sense of loss hadn't diminished.

But now, at least, she could show Giovanni what Alberto was made of and how little he could be trusted—with family money at least. She'd keep his crimes against herself quiet. It was too late to help Alberto's newest victim. But the sooner she finished her job the sooner she could let Giovanni get on with his life without her.

Giovanni's response to her pathetic attempt to seduce him had obviously been purely automatic. What he really wanted she couldn't give him—trust—and he'd fallen out of love with her. Whatever his real purpose in bringing her to Italy had been, it hadn't been to rekindle their relationship. That much was clear. She knew when she left it would be for good and he wouldn't follow her again.

She flipped open her laptop and logged into the company's security system. The sooner she'd finished gathering the evidence that would put Alberto away, the sooner she could leave.

She felt the storm's heavy atmosphere all around her, isolating her from the world. Rain and wind battered her windows and darkness enveloped the palazzo. She'd never felt so alone.

IT WAS past four in the morning before he saw the light dim from her window. He sat watching the nightlife high above Milan, aware of her working across the courtyard. He knew what she was doing. Working to forget. It was the one constant in her turbulent childhood—her studies, her work —the one thing on which she could rely. That was what she'd always done. He could read her like a book.

It was her lack of understanding of him that had always perplexed him. For someone so clever, so bright and so understanding in many ways, she didn't know him. He turned away from the window and closed his eyes. Or she didn't dare to know him. Opening up to someone made you vulnerable. He knew that. And she'd have to learn it if they were to be together. And they *would* be together.

Tomorrow. He'd show her tomorrow. He'd make her see.

～

"Come, I have something to show you."

Rose looked up blinking at Giovanni, standing over the computer.

"I'm busy."

"Firstly, it's Sunday. Secondly you've not stopped all day and you were up most of the night working."

"How did you know?" She looked around the office and blinked. It was empty. "Hey, where is everyone?"

"You must be the only person in Milan who doesn't know that it's the Festa del Naviglio today.

"Ah," she rubbed her eyes, smarting from looking at the computer screen all day, "that's why they all had urgent appointments. She looked back at the computer absently. "Look, here, Giovanni, I need to show you—"

"You can tell me as we walk."

She raised her eyebrows and smiled at him. "We're walking?"

"More surprised that we're walking or that I'm forcing you to stop work?"

She laughed. "I don't know. Both are pretty unusual."

"I look after my staff. You should know that."

"Right." She dropped her pen and stood up and stretched. "So you do." She turned to him suddenly, suspiciously. "But not usually at such a personal level. What are you up to?"

"Come with me and find out."

"You're taking me to the festival?"

"En route maybe. But it's not our destination."

He held the door open for her as she grabbed her bag and walked towards him.

"Umm. This is all very mysterious." She narrowed her gaze as she brushed past him, trying to ignore the quickening of her breath as she came close. It was as if a flick switched deep inside whenever he was close. Pity it wasn't reciprocated. She was only a staff member after all.

. . .

ONCE OUTSIDE, Rose looked up at the soft blue sky of a beautiful June day—cleared by the storm of its heavy atmosphere —and breathed deeply.

"You were right," she said slipping her hand through his proffered arm. "It's good to be outside."

As they fell into step, a warm glow—of being, in that moment, in the right place—enveloped her. If she had no future with him, now was enough. She looked up at his face, to fix it into her mind. The crisp clear light of the summer afternoon highlighted Giovanni's handsome features. Olive skin, straight black hair that fell across dark brows, above eyes the color of heated caramel. Long cheek-bones swept more down than across, beneath which his skin was dark with late-afternoon stubble.

It was the face of a man unconcerned with his looks, unaware of their power—an intense man, with an almost permanent frown. And then there were his lips: narrow but beautifully shaped. The tension and passion were held in check by that mouth. Years before, his mouth had seemed fuller, more generous, more given to laughing, to hope.

His dark tailored suit clung to his tall frame in all the right places, perfectly reflecting his innate, effortless style. Unlike his colleagues, Giovanni always gave the impression of a corporate man by accident, under duress, unconsciously stylish. He would rather be elsewhere but was focused on what he had to do nevertheless.

He was her man. And that would never change. The effort in keeping her hand still on his arm was immense. She wondered if the need for him would ever diminish. Somehow she doubted it. They'd walked down the same street years ago and her feelings had intensified, if anything, since then.

She sighed.

"Why are you sighing?"

"A little wistful perhaps."

"Wistful or nostalgic?"

"Ah, you remembered." Her hand tightened, involuntarily, around his arm.

"Of course. This is the way we came when we first met."

"I hardly noticed. I think I would have followed you anywhere."

"That didn't last."

She chose to ignore the not-so-subtle barb.

"Anyway, where are we going? Same place?"

"No. The festival first—and then? Something different."

"We're going sight seeing? That really doesn't sound like you."

"I prefer to think of it as gazing upon immortality."

"An art gallery then?"

"Why are you English so prosaic?"

"Please, no praise—it just comes naturally."

"When you were last in Milan, we were both too busy to enjoy it. Last night you said you knew nothing of its treasures. It's time to rectify that."

"You're educating me then."

"No. You don't need any more education. You've spent your whole life filling yourself with facts and figures and certificates. It's time to look at the emotional side, the spiritual side of Milan."

"What exactly are we going to see?"

"You will soon find out."

He squeezed her arm gently to his side in a gesture of affection that disarmed her. She realized that she really didn't care where he was taking her, so long as she was with him.

.   .   .

It wasn't until several hours later that they'd emerged from Naviglio with its criss-cross of canals and carnival atmosphere. They'd eaten at an osterie serving delicious Lombard cuisine and been entertained by street performers and musicians. But then the sun had dipped behind a building and Giovanni had hailed a cab for the short ride to the Castello Sforzesco.

Despite it being a familiar landmark, Rose had never entered. She'd always been too busy to join the throngs of tourists to check out the treasures within. But today, with the sun lowering in the sky, the fountain spun its rainbows in the sky only for them. The festival had robbed the usual tourist attractions of their crowds, lending a quiet magic to the beautiful buildings.

"The Castello Sforzesco? Why here?"

"You'll see."

"Will we have time? It must be closing soon."

"We're only going to one room. It will not take long. The Sala degli Scarlioni."

She looked up at the Filarete Tower that fronted the massive brick fortress.

"Not bad as ancestral homes go. Is that why you wanted to bring me here? To impress me?"

"It's true it was originally built by my ancestors. But I doubt much is left from the 14th century. And I doubt such a thing will impress you. But I'm hoping what I will show you will."

They walked in silence through the massive Piazza d'Armi past treasures—architectural and artistic—without stopping. Time seemed to stop as soon as they'd entered the building; the traffic was muffled and the outside world rolled away.

It was only when they entered a vast room, with red

zigzag lines running around the top that Giovanni paused. He took hold of her hand and drew her directly to a small sculpture standing in an alcove.

"The Rondanini Pieta. Michelangelo's final sculpture. He was working on it in the last weeks of his life—1564. What do you think?"

"It beautiful. And strange."

She stood silent, looking at the statue, taking in the cool marble lines—its finished and unfinished qualities.

"It's not his usual work, that much is true. It's of the Virgin Mary mourning the dead body of Christ. She has her arms around him, holding him to her."

She moved round to see the statue from the side. "But she looks like she's the one needing the support. Look, it's almost as if he's propping her up. Don't you think?" She turned to face him.

To her surprise he was watching her closely.

"I think you're right. The divine Christ is also a broken man, supportive and yet needing support."

"Well, I guess nobody's perfect—even Christ."

"Some might find your conclusion sacrilegious, *cara*. But, aesthetically? Esattamente. Nobody stands alone. Come, our excursion is over."

They walked out into the Ducal Courtyard and back onto the streets of Milan. The peace and quiet of the Castello Sforzesco were gone and they were once again a part of the busyness of the world.

The peace may have disappeared and so, too, had some of the magic. But Giovanni's message had been as clear as daylight. Told in his inimitable style.

He was asking her to trust him, to lean on him, to have faith in him.

There were a hundred reasons why she shouldn't trust

him and she would have given them to him if he'd simply asked her outright. But he was too clever for that. He wanted her to make an emotional choice, not a logical one.

THE PALAZZO WAS in darkness when they arrived back. Giovanni closed the front door behind them and flicked on the light switch.

"Drink?"

Rose nodded and they entered the formal salon. It wasn't used often but was a beautiful room, particularly at that time of evening when the light was soft and mellow and played tricks on the ornate plasterwork, giving it a depth and mystery. She sat on an overstuffed chaise longue upholstered many decades before in a pale blue and eau de Nil chintz and ran her fingers over the faded silk, as exquisite as all the other furniture.

He handed her a glass of dark red wine and settled in the seat opposite.

"Why are you smiling?"

"At this beauty. It's all around you. I can't begin to imagine what it must have been like to grow up surrounded by such things."

"It was magical. It was normal."

"How can magic be normal?"

He shook his head and took a sip of wine.

"Come, there must have been moments of magic in your life?"

She shook her head. She couldn't even bring herself to say it out loud.

"No fairies, no mermaids, no glittering mirage in which anything could exist, in which your imagination wasn't limited?"

"An imagination was a dangerous thing to have in a council estate in east London. You had to have eyes in the back of your head. My mother believed magic came from a bottle of pills." She shook her head again. "You've no idea, Giovanni."

He frowned. "Everyone needs magic. I will show you some tomorrow."

"Umm. It's so easily conjured up, is it?"

"There is no conjuring involved. It is all around us." He leaned towards her and took both his hands in his. "You simply need showing."

She smiled. He was as irresistible as he was unfathomable.

"How much longer, Rose?"

Distracted by the warmth of his hands on hers and the direction of her thoughts, it took her a minute to understand what he meant.

"How much longer," he repeated, "before you have found the proof you need?"

"Oh!" She sat back, discomfited by the sudden change from personal to business. "Only a few days. I have most of it."

"Ahh. It did not take so long to discover that Alberto is thieving from his own family?"

"No. He hadn't covered his tracks well. I guess he thought his family would never investigate him."

"And he's right. I had an ulterior motive in taking it this far."

"Your dislike of him?"

He grunted. "No, that was not enough. I have disliked him ever since he was a child and tore wings of butterflies." He looked into the distance. "I could never imagine why he would want to do that." Then he looked at her once more. "But then I could never understand him at all."

"Why then?"

"I have my reasons."

"And you don't intend to tell me."

He leaned towards her. "We may still be married in name, *cara mia*, but I do not, nor ever have, told you everything."

"Secrets?"

"There is no harm in secrets, providing they are kept for good reason."

His words brought hope to her heart.

She started forward. "You believe that?"

"Of course."

"Even if it's someone other than you with the secrets?"

"What are you trying to tell me?"

She hesitated. She wanted him to know everything but had no idea what his reaction would be. She risked everything in the telling.

The silence was broken by the massive seventeenth-century grandfather clock chiming the hour—two long, deep tones reverberated around the room. It was ten past nine. The grandfather clock was kept for aesthetic and sentimental reasons only. That was the thing about Giovanni. He had a passionate attachment to those things he loved. She just didn't know whether she was one of those things any more.

"Giovanni? Tell me. Do you believe that Alberto was my lover?"

Silence lay heavy but Rose was determined not to break it.

"I don't know. That is your secret."

She could see the tension in his face, in his body, in the way he held his glass of wine.

"Is it? You have never asked me the question directly so how do you know that I will not tell you the answer?"

"You will tell me what I wish to hear because you are not an unkind person."

"You think I am kind, but a liar?"

He put his wine glass down too quickly and drops of the dark burgundy spilt onto the rosewood table. He stood before her, looking down at her, intensity evident in the grim line of his lips and the flicker of a muscle in his jaw.

"Was Alberto your lover?"

She stood up and tilted her face to his. She wanted to see him clearly when she answered him.

"No. There's no way that I ever—"

He stopped her by putting his finger to her mouth.

"That's all I wanted to know."

"Then you should have asked sooner."

He pulled her to him and kissed her gently on the mouth. She melted into his arms, feeling weak with relief that he'd finally kissed her. The longing for his touch and heat upon her had been building since their last kiss and she was finally able to release some of the tension.

He held her tightly against his body and she could feel everything: from the fastenings of his clothes digging into her breasts to his hardness, showing clearly his equal need for her.

It was enough to make her lose the last shreds of restraint. She deepened the kiss, pulling up his shirt with her hands, feeling the heat from his body against her hands. The sensation of the hairs of his body against her sensitive fingertips triggered a soft explosion inside. She gasped.

But it was an explosion that ignited further heat, rather than lessening it. She felt she was going to go crazy if she couldn't feel his body against hers. She slipped her hands round and began undoing his shirt buttons. She'd never wanted him so badly as at that moment.

It wasn't just physical, though. She knew that the hunger inside stemmed from the fact that she'd told him the truth and she'd been believed.

He reacted strongly, holding her close while their kisses built until they pulled away, his lips seeking out her neck and chest. She arched back giving him freer access as her hands busied themselves with unbuttoning his trousers.

It was then that he stopped. He groaned deep against her chest, she could feel it reverberate. She froze. It was a groan of self control.

"Giovanni?"

He held his hand over hers and pulled it away.

"Not like this."

"What are you doing? You never pull away from me."

"We are not ready for this."

"Speak for yourself. I'm ready." She pulled herself to him.

"No. If we make love now, it would be like putting a plaster on a deep wound. Soothing yes, but not healing."

"You don't want me any more, do you?" Tell me the truth."

He kissed her gently. "How can you say that?"

"Easy. When we were married you couldn't keep you hands off me. But now? The occasional kiss if I force you into it, followed by a freeze. As if you're disappointed you've succumbed."

He shook his head wearily.

She stepped away when there was no further response. "With my work complete I can go now. I still have four months left on the contract. But you surely don't want me here, now I've met my end of the bargain."

"You will go when I say so."

The flash of anger reassured her. The old Giovanni was still there lurking beneath. She wanted to tease it up further. She ran her hand down his chest.

"No I won't. I'll go what *I'm* ready. I may have fulfilled my contractual obligations but there's also some unfinished personal business I need to attend to."

"Really? More secrets you're keeping from me?"

"Darling. So cynical. It is not good in one so young." She pulled his head down to hers and kissed him, long and soft on the lips. Her deep-boned anger at his refusal to make love to her kept her in rigid control this time. "Good night."

CHAPTER 8

*W*alking, endlessly walking and searching. But she couldn't find her.

It was cold.

She had to find her before her baby became too cold. She needed to warm her with her own body.

"*Cara!*" She heard him calling their baby, their beloved, and she stumbled on.

Then doors closed behind her, hands held her briefly.

She felt heat surround her and she relaxed for a while.

But the peace didn't last.

A baby crying, her little face distorted with the hysteria of needing her mother.

"Carina!" Rose tried to cry out in her panic, but no sound came. She tried to move towards her baby but her legs were trapped and unable to move. She heard a male voice call her baby once more and knew it to be Giovanni. She tried to ask him for help but was struck mute as before.

Her hands reached out but there were too many things between them, she had to get to her.

"*Cara*! Wake up!"

She sat bolt upright, panting with the exertion that was only taking place in her dreams. Slowly the room came into focus. A wedge of weak sunshine sliced through the room, leaving the rest in obscurity.

"*Cara*." His voice came softly now. His arm came around her shoulders. She dropped her head in her hands.

"A bad dream," she said weakly.

"It must have been. It was one of your more elaborate sleepwalking efforts."

"I slept walked? Oh God, where did I go?"

Embarrassment filled the place of grief. She stayed close to him to hide her burning cheeks.

"You even managed the elevator and came to me, as was right."

She wanted to lean on his strength. But what if it gave way? She'd have nothing then.

"But you can't help me." The whisper emerged from lips that felt unwilling to move, unwilling to form the words that could simultaneously bridge the gap between them and destroy his future.

Holding her close, he drew her face up to his.

"How can you be so sure?"

"Because some things are finished and you just have to live with the consequences."

"Then let me help you with those."

She couldn't face his searching eyes and closed her own, turning away.

"Why should you? Why would you want to?"

"You don't know?" He stood up, looked down at her for a moment, before walking to the partially open shutters and closing them. In the darkness she couldn't see his expression. "Because you are my wife."

"You've made it plain that just being married isn't a relationship. Why do you want to help me?"

Inside, she was screaming for him to tell her the words she hadn't heard for over two long years: the words she'd thought were gone forever. But perhaps a remnant of his love still survived.

But as he turned, her hopes were extinguished.

"Stay here. Get some more sleep. I'll tell your team you won't be in the office today. And nor will I. I'll be waiting downstairs. Come when you are rested."

"Where are we going?"

"I'll need your report first. And then I will show you why I want to help you."

Business again, no doubt. She slumped back, her heart still racing at the thought of her daughter needing her—and her husband not needing her.

But her daughter was dead.

She turned away from the slim lines of dimmed sunlight that escaped from around the shutters and finally slept on a pillow wet with the tears of a mother in mourning still.

"BRITTLE," was the only word Giovanni could think to describe his Rose as she sat on the opposite side of this desk, going through her report on Alberto's crimes.

Shadows lay beneath—and behind—her eyes.

The one was physical—he could deal with that—the other was harder but he was determined to shed light on it nonetheless.

Her report was faultless and told him nothing he hadn't already guessed. He hardly listened to the damning details. It was on her that his full attention was focused.

She was barely holding it together.

He steepled his fingers and considered her.

She stopped talking, sat back, eyes narrowed. "You're not listening to a word I'm saying are you?"

"Not really. Leave it. I'll pass it to my lawyers and they will set the wheels in motion. It's over for now."

"And you take this news with such equanimity? Your own family. It will drive them apart. Your mother will be devastated."

"No doubt. Not that she doesn't suspect, but I imagine she'll be upset that the truth will be made public. It will force her to recognize that her youngest and dearest son is a thief as well as many other things. Don't be concerned about my family. We are one in name only."

He watched as she kneaded her forehead as if to release the tension that he knew was held within.

"This has all been a farce hasn't it?"

"A reason maybe, but no farce. You've done the job I asked you to do."

"So I can go whenever I choose?"

"Of course. You've always been able to do that. You really should read the fine print in your contracts."

"What?" She jumped up and slammed the file of papers onto his desk and stood there, eyes blazing.

"Surely you realized? I may be Italian but I don't stoop to the old ways of blackmail."

The normally peaceful, double-height room echoed to the sound of her angry footsteps on the parquet floor, pacing away from him. She stopped suddenly and turned back to face him.

"You," she stabbed a finger at Giovanni, "are impossible. I have no idea why I ever married you in the first place; why I ever got myself tangled up in such a dysfunctional family, with such a, such a, well," she paused as she glared at him, her eyes straying around his face before settling on his lips, "with such an *unreasonable* man."

He laughed. "Is 'unreasonable' the best you can do for an insult? It's true I am unreasonable. But, I am proud of that. Because reason is cold. And one should only be cold when one is dead. Not before."

It was her turn to laugh. She dropped back down into the chair.

He was relieved to see the brittle defense shatter and disappear as the tension dissolved.

She shook her head, the laughter fading as quickly as it had arrived.

"I am returning to New Zealand, Giovanni. I have no reason to stay."

He felt the pain, like the heat of ice, burn deep inside, but he controlled it. It would never be easy for him to control his feelings, never easy to think, rather than act, first. But he'd learned in recent months that he was strong enough to do so.

"Go if you must, but not until the end of the week. Give us time to complete the business."

She nodded in agreement. He'd known she would. He'd purposely framed the suggestion in way that would appeal to her rational nature.

"OK. The end of the week." Rose stood up and began to walk away.

"Rose!" She hesitated just outside of the pool of light that surrounded his desk, her expression enigmatic. He thought he knew her but could not read the expression he now saw in her grey-blue eyes, huge in the dim light. "You will be rewarded for your hard work appropriately of course."

"Of course."

"But before you go there are a few things we need to do."

"Like what? Not more sight-seeing?"

Laughter flared in her eyes as she groaned. That was better.

"Come, *cara*. So cynical. It is not good in one so young." The echo of her words of the previous night was deliberate. "But no, no more sight-seeing for the present."

"What then?"

"I said earlier I wanted to tell you the reason why you should let me help you."

The only sound that broke the silence was the sound of the gardener in the courtyard beyond the window.

"Yes?"

"But first we need to eat. You are still too skinny."

"Many women would take that as a compliment you know."

"There are many stupid women in this world, but you are not one of them, thank God."

"Thank you for that vote of confidence. But I can look after myself."

His smile dropped as he watched her walk away.

"Stop fighting me Rose." He didn't react to the confusion that briefly filled her face as she instinctively turned to him. "We will go to Lugano. I want some time alone with you."

She hesitated briefly before closing the door behind her.

Don't fight me Rose, because you won't win. Not this time.

THEY DROVE IN SILENCE, turning off the highway and climbing up towards the northern lakes. As they climbed higher she could see across the Po valley to Milan, stretching out behind them, glittering faintly under a veil of mist in the filtered late afternoon sunshine. The modern tower blocks rose above the mist and gleamed dully. The massive complex of the Duomo, too, was visible, carving up the regular city streets. A city of contrasts; Giovanni's city.

A city she knew to be dear to his heart, but from which he also needed to escape at times. His villa on an island near Lugano provided that retreat for him and, while they'd been together, for them both.

The thought of returning there filled her with pleasure and apprehension at the same time. They'd spent the first week after they'd met on the island—it had been a time of discovery and incredible intimacy. But those times had gone. And she had no idea what the future held, for either of them.

LAKE LUGANO WAS a rich cerulean blue under clear and sunny skies.

After a misty Milan, the vivid brightness of Lugano, with its Mediterranean climate, was stimulating to the senses. It was only half an hour away and yet a world apart in climate and atmosphere.

Geraniums, abundant and vivid, spilled from the window boxes of the cafes and townhouses. The scent of lemon verbena, that tumbled from terracotta pots, filled the air, and light filtering through the golden-topped trees, flickered on the paving stones.

They walked slowly down the steep lanes of the Old Town to the Piazza della Riforma. The café-lined square was only meters away from the lake and was crowded with both tourists and locals. There were more people than usual and Rose remembered it was the week-end of the firework display. She didn't know the reason for the display; it could have been purely for the joy of celebrating the long summer of the Italian lakes. For whatever reason it was staged, people came from miles around to witness the incendiary celebration of summer.

The square was buzzing but Giovanni found a table inside their favorite café by an open window.

Rose looked around her. She'd always enjoyed coming here but, for some reason, she felt uncomfortable. She surveyed the people once more inside the restaurant, before scanning the busy square. But the sun was too bright to see properly. She shivered.

"Anything wrong?"

"Just someone walking over my grave."

"Such a charming expression. You used to enjoy coming here."

She smiled, determined to discard the shadows that seemed to follow her.

"I do. And nothing's changed, which makes it perfect." She looked across the room at the staff. "Same waiters."

"And the same menu." Giovanni dropped the menu on the table and poured Rose a glass of water.

"I guess if things work well, there's no need to change."

Giovanni took a sip of his coffee and sat back in his chair, facing her, his features obscured by the bright light that shone in from the window behind him. "Like good coffee?" .

"There is that."

"The light and scents of the Italian lakes in late summer?"

"And that too."

"What else? What else doesn't change? What else have you missed?"

Rose nibbled a biscotti, sipped the hot, strong coffee and smiled.

"I've missed this whole thing."

"This 'whole thing' being Italy or—"

"*You*. I've missed you Giovanni."

He sat back then. "Finalmente. I wondered how long it

would take you to admit it. Life in New Zealand wasn't so good for you."

"It was just what I needed at the time. It was healing."

He shook his head at that. "It was somewhere for you to hide."

"But you found me."

He raised his eyebrows. "You overestimate your ability to disappear without trace. Would you have ever returned if I had not come for you?"

Would she? She didn't know the answer. She shrugged. "From what I'd heard, you haven't exactly stayed at home, pining for me."

"I take pleasure in the company of beautiful women and I was no longer tied to a wife."

Rose swallowed tightly. "And it was enjoyable?"

"Of course. I don't do anything that isn't enjoyable. Life is too short."

"Then why bother coming for me?"

"Unfinished business."

"Ah yes. Business. I'm surprised you didn't haul me back to Milan at the first sign of Alberto's transgressions. You must have suspected long ago."

"Of course, but I wasn't in a hurry to take it further, until recent circumstances made it a necessity. No, there is other business that prompted me to seek you out."

Rose shook her head, confused. "What other business? Us? You seemed to have replaced me pretty easily."

An enigmatic smile briefly filled his face before fading as quickly.

"I had a chance meeting with an old acquaintance of yours."

She jerked her head and stared at him. "Who?"

"A colleague of yours from your time in Hong Kong. She asked after our child."

He sipped his coffee once more as if he hadn't just landed a bombshell on her.

Unprepared, she felt the blood drain from her veins, and a deadly numbness take its place. She opened her lips to speak but they were dry and refused to form an appropriate reply. For what reply could be appropriate?

"I see you are at a loss for words. I can understand that. However I was not at a loss for words and she happily reminisced about how overjoyed you were when you discovered you were pregnant."

Rose shook her head. "No."

"Sorry. Perhaps I misunderstood. You were not happy?"

"No, I don't believe this." She sat on the edge of her seat. "How, how could you, Giovanni, sit there and—"

Tears threatened and Rose looked up at the ornately pressed ceiling briefly before meeting his gaze, his dark eyes not angry as she'd expected but curious, sympathetic almost.

"Sit there and ask you how you felt when you discovered you were pregnant? Easy. I want to know. How did you feel Rose?"

"I was happy." Rose could feel a tear track down her suddenly over-heated skin. Whatever his reason for admitting his knowledge here and now, there was no way in this world that she could ever deny the joy that she'd experienced when she discovered she was pregnant with Giovanni's child.

"I assume I'm the father?" His voice was quiet and his eyes were calm, devoid of anger, revealing only pain.

"How could you even doubt it?"

"Because I don't know; because you told me nothing. I lived away from you for the last six months—hadn't seen you for the last four. You constantly made excuses. What was I to think? You could have had an affair, got pregnant, the affair went wrong and you left. That is how it appeared." His voice was eerily quiet.

"I don't care about everyone else. What do you believe?"

"You should have told me. Sometimes it's hard to believe the truth when everybody and everything tells you something different. Tell me now."

She took a deep breath and let her words out in a rush.

"Carina died. She was in my body for only a little over seven months. I killed her. It was my fault."

Even though he'd known the facts she could see the effect of her bald statement on him, as color leached from his face. He shook his head as if to bring him back to reality.

"I doubt that."

"Why?"

"How could you hurt your own baby? I know it wasn't planned but you would have been a wonderful mother."

"You don't understand. If I'd found help earlier she might have lived. But I couldn't get to the hospital and I lost her. It was *my* fault."

She turned away and noticed for the first time that the hum of conversation had stopped and all eyes were on her. She must have been shouting but she hadn't noticed: because she was used to living with the shouting in her own head.

It was my fault.

She felt his hand grip her arm and twist it to him, the pain layering onto her other pain.

"Listen to me. You could not have killed your child. You would not have. But something happened that you're not telling me. How could a baby die when it has been well for seven months? What happened? An accident of some kind?"

Rose stood up quickly, feeling trapped, feeling panic rising. She gripped her bag and tried to move but Giovanni still held her arm fast.

"I've got to get out of here."

"And run away again? Keep running whenever you

remember? It will not go away. It will haunt your dreams forever."

"Don't you see?" She pulled herself away from his arm, oblivious to the curious stares. "I'm terrified she'll leave my dreams forever. That my baby will go, that I'll forget her, will forget that we ever had a child." Tears ran unchecked down her face now but she was past caring. "I don't want to forget. And I can't live with remembering."

She slammed, unseeing out of the doors. Within seconds Giovanni was beside her, had pulled her into the relative privacy of a closed shop entrance and held her tightly. He pressed against her, using his whole body—his arms, his legs, his hips—to control her, to stop her from moving, from screaming, from running. She could barely breathe with the heat and total control his muscles exerted over her small frame.

"Let me go!" Her voice was muffled against his chest.

"No."

She tried to wriggle out of his grip and get away, anywhere, so long as she was alone. She needed to be alone, needed him not to see the grief she kept inside.

But his grip simply grew tighter as he pulled her to him, trying to quell her struggle and calm her. She had no chance of escape.

She tried one last attempt to pull away. But frustration and grief emerged in a wail that escaped her lips before she could stop it. Heaving sobs wracked her body as she still struggled to escape and as he fought to hold her. The stronger she tried to wrestle her arms away from his, the tighter his hold grew. And still the sobs kept coming. He was not going to let her run from her grief this time.

She couldn't stop shaking but he held her firm. All thoughts of where she was, who she was with, had gone. She could only think of the child she'd lost.

The emptiness and pain hit her like a wall. She'd pushed it out, held it back with control, with purpose, but Giovanni's cool admission of knowledge had hammered down the defenses instantly. The tears that had been suppressed for so long came in floods, but still he held her.

Slowly she came round. He held her loosely now, stroking her hair, soothing her. She could feel his wet shirt beneath her cheek. She could feel his strength seeping into her, comforting her, upholding her. She wanted to stay that way forever—in a place of comfort from her pain. She knew when the moment was over the pain would return and she'd have to re-build those defenses that he'd so effectively shattered. Because she couldn't do it without him.

Gradually the movement of people and traffic filtered through to her but inside this place of refuge there was only Giovanni with his arms around her, and the ebb and flow of life around them.

Slowly Giovanni relaxed his hold and drew away from her. She could see the dark stain that her tears had made on his shirt and wondered at his compassion for her.

"That wasn't just about Carina, was it Rose?"

She didn't reply, but closed her eyes and pulled away from him, as if to walk towards the lakeside.

But he held her hand tight.

"You're going to have to tell me some time."

She tried to pull away from him.

"You're hurting me."

"Not as much as you're hurting yourself."

SMALL GROUPS of firework displays had already sparked into life as they drove along the lakeside, a taste of the elaborate display to come. Rose watched through the open top of the car as brilliant sparkles of light flung heavenwards with a bang, before crackling as if in delight to find themselves so high in sky, and falling, evaporating into the air as they descended into nothing.

Neither of them spoke and the silence grew heavy and uneasy, laden with need—the need to know the answer to questions not asked, and the physical need for each other that they could hardly keep at bay.

"I'm sorry Giovanni." She looked out the car window, not daring to face him. "I should have told you."

The silence concerned her more than any sharp retort could have done. The only indication that he'd heard what she'd said was a tightening of his grip on the steering wheel. He kept his eyes firmly on the road ahead.

She closed her eyes briefly before turning to him. He was staring at the road ahead as they wound along the shore of the lake.

"Talk to me Giovanni."

"What do you want me to say? Of course you should have told me. There are many things you should have told me. But that's not your style, is it Rose?"

"I have no 'style'. All I have is an upbringing that made it important to keep things close."

"You don't have to any more. You can tell me everything now. You can trust me, you know. You must tell me everything. It's our last chance, Rose."

She nodded. She knew it. But knowing it in her mind was entirely different to feeling it in her heart. Had he really changed so much that she could trust him with something that could destroy him? It was too big a risk to take —even now.

He put his arm around her shoulders and pulled her towards him. "When you're ready. We have tonight."

"Just tell me that you don't hate me for keeping Carina a secret from you, for leaving you without a word."

She waited long minutes before he answered.

"How can you hate the person you adore most in the world?"

She sank against him, heavy with relief, groping for his hand, holding it tight in hers, determined never, ever to let go of it again.

He was right. She'd have to tell him soon.

CHAPTER 9

The boathouse stood alone at the water's edge—a sentinel guarding access to the Visconti islet. Beyond it, despite the fact the sun had not yet set, the formal firework display had begun; an extravagant celebration of color and sound that lent an unreal, picture-book quality to the scene.

Giovanni slammed shut Rose's door behind her and watched as she walked over to the boathouse and looked across the lake. The fireworks exploded their brilliant array of rainbow colors into the sky. He watched as her gaze followed their upward arc until they disappeared in the deepening blue.

The gentle breeze coming off the lake rattled the line of palms that fringed the lakefront and flicked her curls lazily around her shoulders. Despite the faraway noise of exploding fireworks, a sense of peace pervaded the small promontory; the distant hum of traffic somehow emphasized the sense of removal from the world. He watched as she took a deep breath and relaxed her shoulders. It seemed that she felt it too.

He hated himself for making her face up to her pain, but it was the only way he could think to help her move forward.

He slipped his arm around her—allowing his finger-tips to savor the silk of her bare arms—and followed her gaze.

"I'd forgotten how beautiful it was."

Her words were quiet, her nervous energy worn away. She looked tired but more at peace than before.

He looked at the view, through her eyes, and saw its beauty for the first time in years.

The wild, forested shorelines plunged directly into the water and the fading sunlight of the south-facing bay created a vivid contrast to the darkness of the pine forests opposite. In between lay the island—his retreat from the world—the only access to which was by boat.

He turned and kissed her gently on the lips. "Not as beautiful as you, *cara mia*."

She smiled. Her eyes suddenly alight with the reflected shower of brilliant magnesium-white fireworks. "You, Giovanni," she prodded his chest with her finger, "are pure Italian. I must look a wreck."

He shook his head, finding it hard to find the right words to express how he felt. He'd simply have to show her.

"Silenzio. Andiamo!"

He unlocked the boathouse, helped Rose into one of the smaller boats and started the engine.

They sped across the narrow stretch of calm, deep blue water to the island. The golden light of the fading sun spun its magic on the world around them; the mountain that rose majestically on the opposite shore to the mainland was on fire, while its verdant foothills were already in shadow.

Halfway between Lugano in Switzerland and Campione in Italy, the islet had always been a haven from politics and law—its sole habitation having been a monastery.

That sense of retreat existed still.

Within minutes they were drawing up at the jetty, above which curled huge, ancient, gnarled olive trees: their aged grey trunks framing the entrance to the winding pathway that led up to the house.

They climbed the hill along a footpath lined with Cyprus trees, passing through remnants of the monastery gardens with their walled gardens and paved cloisters.

At the top of the path, elevated on a plateau, the villa lay spread before them, its front walls replaced by windows that contrasted with the rough plaster finish of the walls. Giovanni had renovated the villa: simultaneously taking it back in time, to its austerity and simplicity and yet also bringing it into the future with its vast windows and luxurious interior finishes. It had no Visconti history attached to it. It was bought for its inaccessibility and its lack of modern conveniences. No phones, no computer connections, no unwanted interruptions. Just plenty of books, peace and time to reflect.

In the garden, too, fashions had changed over the years and the utility of the monastery gardens had first been transformed into a structured garden of terraces and symmetry. This, in turn, had given way to the rambling, overgrown English style of garden. The terraces that climbed up to the centre of the island, behind the villa, were now overgrown, wild with thyme and rosemary, herbs once grown by the monks for their healing properties.

Rose needed time to heal and he didn't intend to rush her.

The household staff had left the island earlier, as instructed. They had the place to themselves. He led her onto the terrazza and pulled her to him. She rested her head against his chest and they sat in silence, listening to each other's heartbeats, sensing and experiencing the peace of being together. They watched the lights flick on one by one in the long twilight in the villages that dotted the shore of the mainland. Splashes of bougainvillea and brightly-colored geraniums seemed to glow in the fading light. And they watched the fireworks over the lake gather momentum and climax in a spectacular explosion of color, light and sound.

Giovanni didn't know how long they sat together: one of his arms holding her close, the other stroking her hand. But he did know that he'd never felt so close to anyone in his life. It was dark now and he dipped his head and kissed her gently on the top of her head.

"Rose," he called softly. But there was no movement. Her breathing was soft and regular. She was fast asleep. He smiled to himself. It wasn't exactly how he'd planned to spend the evening. He lifted her gently into his arms and took her inside the villa, lay her softly onto their bed and covered her with a quilt. The nights could be cool. And it didn't look as if he'd be warming her tonight.

ROSE AWOKE WITH A START. She stretched, realized she was still fully clothed and grinned. So, their evening hadn't gone to plan. But, here she was, the sun streaming into the room, alone with Giovanni on the island.

Yesterday she'd felt drained after discovering Giovanni had known about Carina. Today, after a good night's sleep she felt nothing but utter relief. He'd discovered one of her secrets and he'd understood. She would tell him everything today. It was now or never. He'd understand; he'd said he would. And she felt the truth of his words in her heart.

She just had to find him.

THERE WAS no sign of him in the huge open-plan living room that was flooded with light from its eastern windows. In the kitchen, she poured herself a coffee before wandering into his study. Still no sign. Pushing open the back door she walked outside, into the walled garden.

Espaliered fruit trees lined the walls and bees hummed around heavily scented flowers that tumbled in profusion. Head height hedges divided the garden further and it was from behind one of these that she could hear Giovanni's voice.

"I'll leave it to you. I'll give you the evidence you need. Just make sure you use it."

"Giovanni?"

She stepped into the quiet of the small herb parterre. Giovanni looked up at her briefly and then clicked his cell phone shut.

"What's going on? Anything I should know about?"

She waited a few moments for him to speak.

He didn't.

"Are you going to tell me?"

He glanced at her briefly, his look enigmatic, unreadable.

"It's about Alberto."

"Giovanni. I know about Alberto. I know why he hasn't been around. I'm sorry for your family—despite everything he's still your brother, but I do know."

"Ahh. I wondered if you'd heard. I'd wanted to keep it from you."

"Why? You know that I have no love for him. Or even liking come to that."

"It was rape. The most despicable of crimes—using a man's power against a woman. I wanted to protect you from such violence."

She swallowed. She could see the anger rise in him at the thought of her in connection with such a crime. How could she tell him? What would he think of her if he knew of the attack and knew that she'd tried to save her child by not fighting back?

She swallowed hard.

"You can't always protect me."

"I can try. I've failed in the past. I won't fail you again." He dropped the cell phone onto a wooden bench. "The date of his trial has been set."

"He's still out on bail?"

"Si. But his court case begins tomorrow."

"What's the likely outcome?"

"If he's found guilty—and I understand he will be—then he will be imprisoned for a long time. Probably not as long as he deserves."

"They have all the evidence they need then."

He nodded. "And the evidence you uncovered makes a direct connection to the victim's family. It was a pre-meditated attack, not only on the girl but it was also a form of revenge on her family, who'd offended him in some way. Your evidence will show the connection and will ensure he receives the maximum sentence. We still need your final report, but I've advised them verbally of its contents."

She felt stupid. She hadn't made the connection. Hadn't known the identity of the victim even. But it all fitted together.

"You brought me over from New Zealand in order to make sure that Alberto didn't escape his crime?"

He nodded. "I've had my suspicions for a while but this time it was worse and he needed to be punished for his crimes; made to realize that he is the only one responsible for his actions. I knew the girl's testimony alone wouldn't do it. Alberto's lawyers were the best money could buy—the best my family's money could buy. But now? He won't be free for many years."

She bent down and smelled a heavily scented old-fash-ioned violet rose, in an attempt to hide the effect his news had on her. She couldn't believe it—the specter of Alberto returning and destroying her fragile, uneasy truce with Giovanni had just vanished. Giovanni had no idea what he'd just given her.

Freedom.

It was as if a weight had lifted from her.

She took a deep gulp of the sweet soft air that filled the enclosed garden and laughed with sheer joy.

"You, Signore Giovanni Visconti, are one formidable foe. Remind me not to ever have you as my enemy."

"There is no chance of that mia carenna."

"You sure?" she teased coquettishly.

"I do not make love to my enemies."

"And you haven't made love to me in over two years."

"Then it is time to remedy that."

GIOVANNI PULLED Rose to him and kissed her, hard. She felt his urgency in every fiber of her being. It had been too long. Gone was the time for waiting, for testing each other, for explanations. There was nothing left but pure need.

His mouth was hungry and demanding. All the emotion that had been simmering under the surface, day in, day out, erupted and was concentrated in that kiss. She could feel his need for her in every twist of his tongue and every caress of her lips. His grip upon her arms was too firm, too strong, but it didn't hurt so much as awake her from the world where she only existed. It brought her to him, enmeshing his needs with her own until she didn't know where one ended and the other began.

Finally they parted. Giovanni let go of her arms and stood back, breathless.

"Get in the house. Now."

She made to move but had second thoughts, a slow grin spreading across her face. "Hey, you can't tell me what to do."

"Rose, if you don't go inside now, I will take you here, in broad daylight."

Her lips twitched. "And that would be bad because?"

He narrowed his eyes and pulled her to him once more.

But he didn't kiss her this time.

Slowly, he unbuttoned her top. He pulled it open and rubbed his thumbs up and over her nipples, still covered by her bra, sending corresponding shivers of sensation curling through her body, like flames licking and teasing her nerve endings until they sparked alight. An involuntary gasp escaped her lips as heat and sensation met and swirled deep inside her. His eyes never left hers but his mouth curled into a very male, satisfied smile at what he saw in her eyes.

He deftly unclipped her bra and lathed each nipple with his tongue.

Then he pulled back and looked at her again, a smile hovering on his lips.

She wondered if the pulse that was hammering in her neck was as visible as her hard, and now wet, nipples. He was still holding her gaze as he popped open the buttons on her jeans and pushed them down off her hips.

Rose stepped out of them, feeling the blush of the early morning sunshine upon her skin.

Their bodies and lips met and formed around each other, blending and merging like two pieces of a puzzle, two opposites finding respite in their opposing force, finding a rightness in their togetherness that was absent when they were apart.

They pulled apart and Giovanni, slowly, gently, lowered her onto a soft bed of chamomile grass, crushing it and bathing them in its fresh scent. He held himself above her as he sought her lips once more, his fingers, hesitantly at first, touching her shoulder, her arm, her hips, her stomach. It was as if he was discovering the curves and softness of her body for the first time.

Moved by his tenderness, Rose kissed his face, his eyes, one by one, touching the features she so loved with her lips. Then she returned to his lips. As his body pressed lightly down on hers, the kiss deepened and became more urgent.

She tore away the buttons from his shirt until it hung free and her hands could touch the skin that she so adored— smooth and taut across his muscles. She could feel them flex as he moved over her, caressing her as she was caressing him.

She pulled away from his lips and, instead, wriggled down beneath him and kissed his chest, inhaling his scent deeply. Then she moved again, feathering her kisses lower until she reached his jeans. Shakily she tried to undo them. But it was too difficult, his arousal too strong.

"Merde!"

Within seconds he'd shaken off his shirt and jeans and was on top of her once more. His mouth descended to her breasts; her nipples peaked and desperate for his touch.

But there was no teasing, no hesitation this time. Giovanni was as desperate to taste her as she was to be tasted. Together they feasted: he, on the sensory explosion of the feel of her nipple in his mouth, of the fragrance of her skin; she, on the deep sensation that his tongue, his teeth and his lips created on her body and that flowed through her until it made an intimate physical and emotional connection deep inside.

She arched her back, pulling away and increasing the tension that shot waves of delicious shivers through her body. Her gasp was cut short by his mouth on hers in a kiss in which all the longing and need of years of emptiness were expressed.

Never before had Rose felt such a suspension of thought, such an overpowering need to claim intimacy with someone.

It was the destruction of the final barrier between them, an affirmation of their love.

But he stopped before she was ready. Pulling away his mouth from hers, his gaze sweeping her body briefly as he pushed her legs open with both his hands and ran a finger inside the scrap of silk that was all that was left of her clothing, leaving it there for one tantalizing second, during which Rose thought she'd explode with need.

Her breathing came short and hard. And then he pulled down the only barrier that was left between them, his hand returning to explore the flesh now unclothed and so obviously needy.

Rose felt a pulse of moisture escape.

She moaned and he lowered himself onto her and kissed her again. There was no gentleness in this kiss, however. No diffidence in his touch.

They knew each other's bodies intimately and responded instinctively: touching and caressing; circling, turning in each other's arms, as one. Without knowing when they joined, only knowing its rightness, they moved together.

She wrapped her legs around him and he moved into and against her repeatedly. It was as if he were trying to break down any barriers between them—reducing them to one element. All she could do was hold on to him as they both came together in explosive release.

SOME TIME later they both lay back, naked in the crushed chamomile, the hot sun heating their sweat-slicked bodies.

There was nothing in the world that could come between them now.

Rose watched as the lightest of clouds trailed across the sky from the west, darkening their bodies momentarily. She frowned as she felt the wind change and a cool breeze flicker across her stomach and breasts.

WHEN SHE AWOKE MUCH LATER in the bedroom, it was dark in the house. The only lights came from the opposite shore of the lake. The windows were open to an oncoming squall and rain had fallen on them in their bed.

But it wasn't the rain that had awoken her.

His fingers gently trailed up her leg, to her stomach, caressing her breasts before rising to cup her face in his hand.

He pulled her towards him, encircling her in his arms, as she snuggled into his chest and closed her eyes, almost purring with an intoxicating blend of satisfaction and desire as he continued to feel her and caress her with his hands and his body.

"I love you Giovanni."

"I know you do."

"You are one conceited man."

"No. There is no point in pretending. We were always meant to be together. It just took you time to make you see it."

"Are you calling me slow?"

"Ah, tesorina mia." He kissed her hair, her cheek, her lips. "Slow, but worth waiting for."

"The thing you may not know about us slow, but steady, girls, is that we have staying power."

"Is that so?"

She wriggled around him, stroking up between his legs with her nails.

"Indeed."

Rose smiled with satisfaction as he entered her once more.

"You are not suggesting that us more fiery types do not have staying power?"

"You know me, I always need proof."

"Then you shall have it."

"On my terms." She smiled as she twisted around until she was seating astride him, still connected.

"I will let you play for a while, *cara*. But when you wish to be serious, let me know."

She eased herself up, off him, and held herself there before sitting fully on him once more.

He groaned and turned her around until she was on her back with no place to go, but under.

"Now, Giovanni, now."

Their gaze met and didn't stray, intent on experiencing their passion through each other, obliterating all other experience, all other thought. All they could be was in this moment with each other, each giving and receiving, exchanging the essence of each other.

Then she closed her eyes and cried out in ecstasy as her body flexed around him, bringing him to his own climax, deep inside her.

Slumped around each other, spent of emotion but still intimately entwined, they lay for a long moment until slowly thought and feeling returned.

THE NIGHT DEEPENED and grew more wild. Rain thundered down on the windows and roof, muffling their words and echoing their cries. Lightening periodically lit the room, casting an icy white light over their sweat-slicked bodies.

And still their lovemaking continued.

The more they discovered about each other, the more each was willing to give and surrender to the other.

Giovanni was right, this was just the beginning of their passion—a passion that seemed without limit.

THEY LAY QUIETLY TOGETHER, listening to the storm raging outside and within, she in his arms.

"No more secrets Rose."

Whether it was an order or a desire, she couldn't tell.

"No more secrets," she whispered—her words expressing more a wish, than a promise.

IT WASN'T until much later that Giovanni felt Rose's limbs relax completely and her breathing quieten and deepen.

The storm was dying, still punctuated with gusts of wind that rattled the windows and distant crackles of thunder. But Rose lay sated and peacefully asleep. Her body relaxed and in total abandon, arms flung wide, a leg wrapped around his.

Giovanni smiled. It made him deeply happy to see her relaxed, without the stresses and worries that made her sleepwalk; no defensive posture, indicating her guard was up; just the essence of the lady he loved. She'd opened herself up to him and he'd gladly taken what she had to offer.

Giovanni wrapped a stray lock of her hair around his finger and kissed it. He felt his heart beat solidly within him and could see the faint movement of the thin skin at her wrist pulse with her life beat, in time to his own. Her delicacy and her strength overwhelmed him.

He traced a fingertip across her breast, watching her skin rise in goose bumps and the nipple pucker in response to his touch. She was exquisite and he couldn't get enough of her.

She sighed and moved her head closer to his, seeking out his presence in her sleep. Her hair tumbled over the pillow and onto his chest. He closed his eyes and buried his face in her hair, inhaling her and holding her there—wanting to keep that way forever.

He concentrated all his senses on the feel of her even breath on his cheek.

Hours passed, intensely savored, until he, too, drifted into a dreamless sleep.

CHAPTER 10

*D*awn broke dull and drained into the uncurtained bedroom. The storm had blown out leaving a strange yellowish light over the lake and forest.

Rose's body felt at ease and relaxed, despite a severe shortage of sleep. When she'd not been dozing, she'd either been watching, or making love to, Giovanni. She'd had too many years without him—nights when she'd cried herself to sleep because she couldn't remember his face. She was determined to imprint every inch of his face and body into her memory this time. Just in case.

Gently she teased her body from his grip and walked over to the window. It was the same view as yesterday but her life had changed forever. Her present and her future were with him now.

She turned to look at him. He lay unmoving, the covers pushed to one side, revealing his body softly shadowed in the dim light.

She could appreciate his beauty now that her body was satisfied. Last night the intensity of their love-making had been all encompassing; there had been no room for thought, for mental processes of any kind. But in that strange light of day, she wanted to experience him at a different level, one that was separate from the night's passion.

She walked quietly up to him looked first upon his sleeping face: relaxed and beautiful. It was always beautiful but it was usually overwhelmed by the strength of his character. This morning, however, the worry lines around his eyes had faded, as had the tension surrounding his mouth. The arrogance and dominance had disappeared and the inner man was revealed, not the man that his family and his fate had made him. She moved to touch him but stopped short. Instead she retreated and reached for her robe.

She frowned as she slipped it on.

She'd lied.

There was still one more secret she hadn't shared. One more, which would hopefully become unimportant in a few days once the trial was over. Only then could she relax fully, knowing the threat of Alberto had disappeared.

In the meantime she had to push it to the back of her mind. Nothing could come between them, their love was too strong.

She leaned out the window, breathing deeply of the fresh, morning air. Beneath the open window was a drift of white scented flowers that were almost luminous in the dull light. Despite the niggling worry, everything—from the beauty of her surroundings to the satisfied languor of her body— reminded her of the absolute joy she'd found in Giovanni's arms.

It was as if they'd never been apart but for one thing. But surely one secret wouldn't hurt. Particularly when the only other person who knew it was to be incarcerated for years. Giovanni would very possibly never find out. The truth need never surface. She need never have to face giving Giovanni the painful news about what his brother had done.

But what if something went wrong? What if Alberto was acquitted and Giovanni discovered everything?

She withdrew from the window as the morning chill began to penetrate her robe. It wouldn't happen. She couldn't let it. She'd make sure her report gave Alberto's prosecution as much ammunition as she could find.

She picked up her hairbrush and began to beat her hair into submission.

It wouldn't happen.

Once dressed in the smart work clothes Milan society demanded, she stepped back into the bedroom.

"Come here." The voice was sleepy but the command was unmistakable.

She perched on the side of the bed and held out her hand to him.

He grabbed it and held it tight.

"Why are you up so early? The meeting isn't until this afternoon."

"It's OK for the boss to laze around but the workers have work to do this morning."

"Leave the completion of the report to your team. They can do it. I need you here."

"No. I have to finish this. I need to."

There was something in the tone of her voice that made Giovanni sit up and take notice.

"Why?"

"Because there's too much riding on it."

A dull ache settled in his gut.

He noticed then, that she was dressed for work; that she'd slipped back, away from him, into her professional mode. He also noticed how her glance barely rested on him.

The ache turned into something much worse.

The dull light was suddenly sharpened by a ray of sunlight that had broken through the gloom. It illuminated her hair, creating a halo of light, within which he could see no detail.

"Come here. Closer."

She stepped away. "Look, I have to get back this morning. I've arranged for Guido—on the mainland—to pick me up. You stay here, relax. I'll see you later this afternoon."

He lay back, numbly, trying to fight the feeling that Rose had just slipped away from him again. He heard the distant hum of the motorboat approach.

"We'll both return this morning. You can finalize your report—we'll need it for the courts—and I'll catch up with my work before this afternoon's meeting. I'll tell Guido that you don't need the lift. I'll take you. We'll return together. There'll be no more parting."

THE HEAT of the sun had burnt off the remaining strands of murky haze that clung to the lake, leaving the air clear and fresh—full of possibilities.

Sitting beside Giovanni, holding his hand and watching the soft pink of early morning dissolve into rainbow hues through the breaking waves, Rose thought she'd never seen anything more beautiful. If only there wasn't the specter of Alberto hanging over her. Just forty-eight hours to get through and then all would be well.

THE RETURN DRIVE PASSED QUICKLY. Lost in her own thoughts, Rose was relieved that Giovanni didn't question her any further on her change in mood. She tried not to let it show, but it seemed that he sensed whatever was on her mind.

Soon. The need for secrecy, for fear, would be over soon.

WHEN THEY PULLED up outside the Palazzo, Rose could see tension once more in Giovanni's face.

"I'll wait."

She smiled. "I'll be fine. Besides you need to prepare for the meeting as much as me." She felt a flutter in her stomach looking at his frown.

"It doesn't feel right, leaving you alone."

"Come on. After today, we need never be apart. I promise."

"Si certo. I'm never letting you out of my sight again."

"Just this once. It's too important—you need to prepare and so do I. I'll see you in one hour."

"That means two."

She laughed at the scowl on Giovanni's lips and reached over to kiss him. It was meant to have been a peck but Giovanni slipped his hand around the back of her neck and the kiss became long and passionate. She shifted back into her seat and moaned under his lips, her hands slipping into his hair and pulling her hard to him.

He pulled away, his eyes dark with desire.

"I'm coming with you. I want you."

"You always want me." She felt the thrill of knowledge and sureness of his love as she'd never done before. "But you mustn't. Let me prepare myself—go over the findings once more—and I'll be in the office before you know it to brief the team. It's too important."

"Go then, but be in my office at ten. We'll go over the report with the team together. And Rose?" She turned to face him, ready to close the door. "Don't be late."

"As if." She laughed and hopped out. "Not for this meeting anyway." She slammed the door closed and watched as Giovanni roared down the street in the black Maserati.

She couldn't be late for this morning's meeting. Everything had to be right for this afternoon when they met with the board of directors and all the family. Except Alberto of course. He was stuck in Switzerland awaiting trial. He wasn't allowed to leave the city, let alone the country.

Just as well, she thought as she entered the empty entrance hall. She wasn't sure that she would be able to do what she had to do, if Alberto was there.

As much as she hated the elevator for its noisy instability, she pressed the button. With the work still in progress on the winding attic stairs, it was the only means of access. She looked around at the mausoleum of a house.

She'd be pleased to leave it and make her home somewhere else—somewhere new to them both. There was too much history here—centuries of it in fact. They both needed somewhere different to start afresh.

Then it struck her. The lift was taking its time clunking its way down to her. *Down?* It was usually sitting in the basement. She shrugged. Perhaps the workmen had used it last.

On reaching the attic, she swept the grille aside and walked out into the suite of rooms. The neutral colors were bathed in the morning light giving the room a vibrancy and life that the rest of the house didn't share. She flung her bag on the table and quickly plucked out a different suit from the dressing room. If you're going to alienate your mother-in-law and accuse your brother-in-law of large-scale theft, you may as well look smart.

She switched on the shower and went over to the desk—a slab of pale wood in front of the window—to gather together her papers. She reached into her briefcase to withdraw her laptop and her heart missed a beat.

It was empty.

It had been there just the previous day. She looked around, suddenly freaked, panicking. She paced up and down, searching the closets, the cupboards, bags, everything. But it had disappeared. What the hell? She had back-ups of course, but everything she had was on that computer. She would never have left it here except for the state-of-the-art security system that Giovanni had installed.

She switched off the shower and returned to the bedroom, pulling out her clothes one by one and throwing them on the bed.

She must have left it at work. She reached over to pull her cell phone out of her bag but that wasn't there either. Was she going crazy? She'd had the damn thing only moments before.

"Here, is this what you're looking for?"

She screamed and jumped away as a hand touched her waist.

"Alberto!"

"Rose!" He said in mock surprise, echoing her tone. "Whatever are you doing here?"

"You know what I'm doing here." She tried to stem the shaking, tried to control her voice but she could hear the shock and trembling that would indicate weakness to Alberto.

"Are you scared of me, little Rose?" He reached out and tried to stroke her hair. She pulled away. She had to be stronger.

"Why would I be scared of you?"

"Because I've hurt you before and I've spent the time since we last met very profitably, enjoying myself, honing my skills, if you like to think of it that way."

She shook her head.

He smiled. "No, I don't suppose you would."

"My cell phone please." She held out her hand while standing as far away from him as possible.

"Come and get it." He grinned, dangling the cell phone between his fingers.

She held her hands together in an effort to stem the shaking and then lunged for her phone. Surprised he gave it to her, she shakily moved away and pressed in the quick dial number for Giovanni, watching Alberto all the time.

The phone didn't work.

Alberto laughed.

"I'm afraid your SIM card has just gone out the window." He sighed in mock sympathy. "Come sit on the bed with me and talk."

"There's no way I'm going anywhere near you." She strode over to the lift.

"No point I'm afraid. Unfortunately the lift isn't working at the moment. Missing a vital part."

"Don't tell me, it's a vital part that you have on you."

"So quick, *cara*."

She flinched at the use of the word that Giovanni used for her, but remained silent.

Alberto smiled, his eyes cold and calculating. He walked around her, a complete circle. "I thought you might come."

She shook her head and backed off from him, to the window.

"I watched you and my brother going out to the island." He looked at her with mock surprise. "Had you forgotten that I was confined to Switzerland? Lugano, is in Switzerland remember."

"You watched us?" Rose couldn't believe it. The specter of Alberto had been real. He'd been there, watching her when she'd been at her most vulnerable.

"Yes. Very touching too. A bit too emotional for my taste though. Anyway, I thought to myself, how easy it would be to take one of the boats from the boathouse and slip across, unnoticed back to Italy. Back to the palazzo where I could gather your files and disappear. Then you'd have nothing."

"I have back-ups."

"At the office? Ah, Allegra seemed quite happy to give them to me. Such a persuadable girl."

"You didn't hurt her?"

"I didn't have to." He stepped towards her. "I have everything I need to stop you from blackening my name. I'm innocent."

"No you're not. You're as guilty as hell."

He laughed. "No. I'm innocent. You have nothing on me now. I hold all the copies of your report. It's a shame for you that my big brother insisted on absolute confidentiality. Even he hasn't seen the final report, has he? Nothing signed; nothing formal that the courts would require."

"How do you know?"

"Allegra was so forthcoming, as I said. So I have all your evidence and, as a bonus, I have you."

"You don't have me." The anger of two years of watching and waiting and hating flamed deep within her and she brought up her fist to punch him but his hand, more quickly than she'd imagined, shot up and stopped her blow. His fingers squeezed around her arm tightly, cutting off all feeling.

"You didn't fight so much last time did you? I remember."

Rose felt sick at the reminder.

"Perhaps you enjoyed it, despite your pretty remonstrances."

"I had a baby to protect." She spat the words out.

"Ah, but no more." He slid his hand up her arm. "But perhaps in the future?"

She struggled to free her arm.

"There's no point in trying to get away. There's going to

be no-one coming to your rescue, my little English slut. The meeting isn't until this afternoon. That's hours away. You won't be missed until then and, by that time, I'll be long gone. And so will all your evidence."

"I need air."

He flicked her away as if she were worthless and turned his back on her as if to underline the point.

She slowly stepped back until she could feel the catch of the window beneath her fingers. Desperate, she balled her fist and punched it for all she was worth into the glass and screamed.

There was only a dull crack as pain shot through her fingers.

"Good try." He clapped his hands as he approached her. She scrambled with the latch once more.

But he was quicker and she screamed for all she was worth, hoping that the sound would carry through the cracked window, down into the street. The sound stopped abruptly as he grabbed her around the waist, winding her.

He picked her off her feet and threw her onto the bed. Her head hit the corner of the large granite lamp base with a sickening thud. Dizzily she brought her hand up to her head and felt the warmth of the blood. She looked up at him—two of him. He was advancing towards her and she tried to move, to stand, to do anything. But sickness and darkness threatened. Despite the adrenalin rush of panic, the darkness won. The last thing she remembered was the sweet smell of his aftershave as his body touched hers.

"Where the hell was she?"

She'd said she wouldn't be late and he'd told her the meeting was at ten. It was, in fact, later, but she wasn't to know that. He'd needed some excuse to get her back to him early.

It was now ten past eleven and there was no sign of her. She was always one hour late—no more and no less. He'd sometimes reckoned her body clock was in a different time zone—one of her own making. But, whatever, it wasn't like her.

Something was wrong.

And where the hell was Allegra? She'd disappeared off the face of the earth. What the hell was going on?

He double-clicked icons madly, trying to work out where things had been filed. It was all too logical—he didn't understand it. He couldn't find a thing.

His staff didn't know—hadn't been involved because of the secrecy—and were running around trying to appease him. It was driving him mad.

"Let me have the mouse, sir, I'll try to find what you're looking for."

"Here," he yanked the mouse from its connection and tossed it to one of his executives. Then he took the laptop and pitched it in the wastepaper bin.

"You find her work. I want it here—on paper—when I get back."

Within minutes he was in his car driving back to the Palazzo. He'd felt strange earlier on, leaving her by herself. He cursed himself. He shouldn't have listened to her. He'd always worked on gut instinct and he should have followed it then.

The car bounced over the potholes and juddered as he sped over the paved streets in the old city. He blared his horn at a group of young people, not a care in the world, who were dancing in the square, stopping all traffic. Cars tried to overtake and he was soon hemmed in—stuck with nowhere to go.

Damn. The phone went suddenly. He glanced at the screen. Allegra.

He listened for a few moments.

"How long since he was last seen?"

He cursed roundly, furious with himself, and threw down the phone.

Icy anger filled his veins. He revved the engine and drove between cars, turned around and sped off the wrong way down a one-way street.

GIOVANNI LOOKED BRIEFLY UP at the Palazzo Visconti. The window was cracked. He jumped out of the car and ran up the front steps.

Then he stopped. There was none of the usual signs of Rose's occupation: no window open, no sounds of opera. Only silence. Something must have gone wrong.

He entered the palazzo stealthily, his mind racing, his body moving quietly, with deliberation. Once inside he pressed the lift. Nothing. No whirring sound, no movement. Quietly he pulled open the grille and saw the bottom of the lift was stuck on the upper floor.

The sight made him sick with fear. He started to run for the stairs but cursed, remembering they didn't yet exist—still under repair.

Then the cold realization hit him. Rose was in the attic suite with Alberto and there was no way in.

HE WAS ABOUT to slam his fist into the lift but stopped. That would only alert Alberto to his presence—if he didn't know already.

He had to think.

The attic. There had to be other ways to access the attic.

He closed his eyes with relief when he remembered. He had a vision of darkness and safety; the smell of mothballs, decaying papers and wood; the sound of scurrying rodents. But, above all, he remembered the feelings of safety when, as a young boy, he'd climbed from attic to attic, to get away from the violent arguments of his parents. He was safe because no-one, including his younger brother, knew about how the attics opened one upon another—a throwback to the war in case of invasion—to enable people to move around unseen.

He turned round and quietly closed the front door.

"AWAKE YET?"

Rose groggily sat up in bed. She'd been stripped down to her underwear and was lying, covered by a sheet, in bed.

Her head pounded and she tentatively felt the encrusted blood. She swallowed dryly. A strip of towel had been tied tightly around her mouth as a gag. She tried to scream.

"What are you trying to say? I can't hear you. Just lie back and enjoy because you're not going anywhere for a long time. I've been very patient waiting for you to wake up. You know, I don't like it when people are mean to me. And you were mean to me, weren't you, that last time? First you wouldn't let me kiss you. And then I had to make you. Second not wanting me to make love to you. And then, well, we didn't quite make it that far did we? Shame. Still, I helped out old Giovanni with getting rid of the baby. He should be thanking me, not trying to frame me.

Rose brought herself up on the bed but had to lie down again because the room was spinning. Slowly Alberto came into focus. It was the first time she'd really looked at him. He was the same, smoothly handsome man, all golden hair, golden skin and broad, white smile. The same, that was, except for his eyes: his pupils were dilated and his eyes shifted constantly and his hands shook. She recognized the signs instantly from her mother. She wondered how long he'd been hooked; whether his early attempts at violence were because of drugs or the drugs were in response to his perversions.

"And then, you top the insults off by trying to prove that I've been stealing from the family. What that's to do with you, I've no idea. You're a nobody. Always was and always will be. You're simply useful to my brother. I mean, you can't think he loves you. It's obvious he only came to get you when he needed you. Not before, did he? Now don't look like that."

She tried to wriggle away from him but he pinned her down with his arms, and the throbbing of her head increased until she thought she'd faint again. She needed to remain conscious.

"I want to see your mouth Rose. Promise me that you won't make a noise."

She nodded. He reached over and undid the scarf and she took a deep lungful of air and screamed.

She didn't feel the pain of his blow until several minutes had passed, disguised as it was by the existing pain.

Alberto turned her to face him and she could do nothing else but what he asked. She was too weak to fight him any longer. She could see the features, similar to Giovanni's but diluted in their fleshiness and insipid in their coloring. He was a shadow of a man.

Then time seemed to slow.

At the same time as the sound of splintering wood reached their ears, panic and fear filled Alberto's eyes.

Shouts and voices, more than one, filled the room and Alberto was hauled off the bed by unknown arms.

She moved then, risking unconsciousness, to see who the arms belonged to. Five policemen surrounded and held

Alberto. Behind them, surrounded by other policeman stood Giovanni, his face livid with anger.

"Giovanni?"

Pray God he wouldn't do anything stupid and endanger himself. She couldn't lose him now.

"Rose." He was beside her in an instant, gently touching the places where she'd been hurt—her cheek, her chin. She saw the blood on his hands. There mustn't be any more.

"Giovanni. Don't," she winced as he touched the open wound with a cloth one of the officers had given him.

"Shush, don't speak. Let me deal with this."

"No. Don't do anything. Don't hurt him, Giovanni."

Giovanni looked at Rose in disbelief. And then he looked up at his brother and stepped back. He wanted to hurt him as he'd hurt Rose but more than that he wanted to kill him.

Alberto's scared face melted into a smirk.

"You see big brother, your wife doesn't want me hurt. Isn't that touching? And you thought I had her here under duress. Well, her words say it all."

Rose lay back, white-faced and weak. Giovanni smoothed the blood-matted hair off her face. "Did he do anything else to you?"

"Just this," she touched her head. "I fell…"

"She fell, you see brother. Why would I hurt my darling sister-in-law."

Giovanni let the pounding in his veins slow before turning to the policemen. "Send for the ambulance."

"They're on their way up, Signore."

Giovanni walked purposefully over to Alberto.

"No Giovanni!" shrieked Rose.

But Giovanni ignored her cries, opened up Alberto's jacket and pulled out the missing lift part. "This will make it easier for them." He handed the part to the police.

He could see Alberto relax with relief. He'd thought

Giovanni was going to hit him. Well, he'd learned a few things since he'd met Rose. He began to walk away.

"She didn't tell you about her and me? About the last time we were together? This isn't the first time you know. I know Rose intimately. We spent her last evening at the Palazzo together. Downstairs in your bedroom."

Giovanni and Rose exchanged glances. All Rose could do was to shake her head.

"But it didn't end nicely for your Rose did it? Poor girl was upset that I didn't want her any more. Looks like she's been trying to get back at me for rejecting her, with all this sleuthing work.

"Shut up Alberto. You're lying. You may have wanted to but you haven't touched her. Rose has told me everything." He turned to her. "Haven't you Rose?"

"Giovanni, I—"

"Haven't you Rose?"

Somehow the pain had turned his voice cold.

Alberto laughed. "You really think it was coincidence that she disappeared after your return from those months overseas? She disappeared because she couldn't bear to be with you after she'd made love to me."

"She has never been with you."

"Yes she has, brother. And very nice too. But, you know? I didn't want your leftovers."

"Rose. Why didn't you tell me?"

But there was nothing but blank shock and pain on her face. It said it all.

Something strong sapped out of Giovanni then and he turned, balled his fist and threw it into his little brother's face. The pain inside dulled the pain of the punch as he left the room.

He turned to the policeman. "Charge me if you must."

"Why signore?"

"I've assaulted my brother."

"None of us saw anything, signore."

Giovanni entered the lift and fell back on the metal cage. As the lift slowly grated its way down to his room, all Giovanni could hear were the pathetic screams of pain from his brother and the quiet sobbing of his wife.

CHAPTER 11

*I*t was the silence that awoke her the first time.

After trying to follow Giovanni out into the night, after refusing to go to hospital and after dismissing the nurse that Giovanni had arranged, the doctor had given her a strong shot of sedatives and pain relief that had knocked her into a long and dreamless sleep.

But then, too soon, the drugs had worn off. It was in the early hours that she'd awoken to hear the sound she'd dreaded—silence.

There was only the hum of the ever-constant traffic; the sudden shout from people returning from a long night of revelry and the distant, repetitive thud of a drum beat. But those sounds were ever present, the background, white noise of city life.

What she wanted to hear—and didn't—was the sound of someone moving close to her; someone's breath flowing in and out beside her ear; someone calling her name.

Not someone, she realized, but Giovanni.

She turned over painfully, the absence in her heart greater than her physical hurts.

She squeezed her eyes closed as if to shut out the pain. But it was contained within. The heavy, humid night air had been as oppressive as the silence.

She'd lain awake for some hours before taking more tablets to numb the pain of her thoughts and heart.

Oblivion had eventually claimed her and now the soft light of morning filtered through her window once more.

The silence was different however.

It was the weighty silence of someone else in the room— someone watching but not speaking—that awoke her.

Her senses prickled with awareness.

"You're there, aren't you, Giovanni?"

She could feel his presence without seeing, or hearing him.

A chair scraped heavily on the floor and footsteps approached the bed.

She closed her eyes with relief.

"You really should stop watching me while I sleep. It's becoming a habit."

She turned and looked up at him, a smile ready on her lips. But he looked worse than she felt. Dark shadows lay below his eyes and his clothes were disheveled and still damp from the morning air. He looked as though he'd been awake all night.

He ignored her attempts at humor. Perhaps he hadn't even heard them.

"How do you feel?"

"My head will recover. That's not my main concern."

She pulled herself up in bed, wincing as her head throbbed with the effort.

He reached over to the medical supplies on the table, soaked some cotton wool and gently blotted away the fresh blood that had sprung up at her temple. But he was too calm, too proficient.

She looked into his eyes, the brown almost charcoal in the cool light of morning. He was so close and yet so distant now. It made her realize that, this time, it was over.

Twice she tried to speak and twice he shook his head, silencing her.

"I have things to do now, Rose. I suggest you rest. I just came to make sure you're OK."

"I'm fine but we need to talk."

"About what? It seems there is little you wish to confide in me."

"It didn't happen as Alberto described, we didn't—"

He brought his hand to her mouth to stop her from saying anything further. "No." He shook his head and walked away. "I don't want to hear any more. The details are unimportant."

"Giovanni. I've tried to tell you before. But I was scared. I tried, Giovanni. It was too difficult."

"It is not so difficult if you really love someone, really trust someone. I think you don't love me enough."

Stunned, the words vanished from her lips. His face was like a mask. Suddenly it didn't seem like him, not her Giovanni. He was talking to her with the same polite, distant manner he reserved for casual acquaintances. The words were a parody of the intimacy they'd once shared. He obviously took her stunned silence for agreement.

"I thought that might be case," he continued. He got up and walked to the door. He shook his head as she tried to follow. "You need to rest. You're still in shock."

"No listen—"

"It's too late."

"When are you coming back?"

He shrugged. "What does it matter to you? Very little it would seem."

"How can you say that?"

"How? Because I have seen nothing to suggest you feel otherwise."

"Come back. I can explain. I need you, Giovanni."

"Need, but not love? I can't live with that." He turned away briefly and she couldn't see his face. But the change in his tone spoke volumes: rasping, emotional, final. He'd gone from her. "Rose, it's so difficult, loving you. I've made so many changes, tried to show you what life could be like if you'd only trust me. And you haven't listened to, or understood, a word. And you're not prepared to make any changes for me. This is not the behavior of a woman in love. You put yourself and your needs first. You're a selfish woman."

"I've *had* to be selfish, Giovanni. My whole life. I couldn't trust my own mother. It was the only way I could survive; the only way to make sure I didn't slip into her dependent ways. If it wasn't drugs, she was dependent on men, even me in the end."

"Don't think I don't understand, Rose, because I do. But you had me. You had *me*, but you didn't seem to notice or care."

She flinched at the past tense.

"It's hard to change. It's hard to feel safe. I still felt there was no-one I could trust more than myself."

"There was our love. Couldn't you even trust that?"

She shook her head. "That night when Alberto…" She trailed off, not knowing whether Giovanni had discovered exactly what had happened that night.

"I know the truth about what happened. It's surprising how a little pain, and the threat of more, loosened my brother's tongue. I'm so very sorry for what he did to you. But you should have trusted me with the truth."

"I know." She looked down, pleating the covers with her fingers, trying to say the words she should have said years ago. "It was just that our love seemed too good to be true, too good to last. Deep down it felt that, somehow, a mistake had been made. Nothing had lasted in my past before, why now? When he attacked me, a part of me thought: yes, that's right, that's how it ends." She looked over at Giovanni but he was gazing fixedly out of the window. "But you're wrong. It wasn't selfishness that stopped me from telling you about Alberto. I did it for you."

He turned to her in disbelief.

"You did it for me? You thought that I needed protecting from myself? That I would endanger myself in some way because of what Alberto had done to you?"

She nodded.

"You think I am a fool, Rose?"

"No of course not. I think you are a passionate man who sometimes allows his passion to over-ride his sense."

He sighed. "Truthfully. I don't know what I would have done. Maybe it would have been as you say. Maybe not. But not to trust me with this? It undermines everything. There is no possibility of a future now. It's gone. You've destroyed it."

She didn't see his face again. He slammed the elevator button, leaned his weight against the grille and waited with his back to her.

In despair she turned away, her head in her hands, her legs slowly pulling up to her chest until she lay curled and sobbing, listening to the lift clank its way down the shaft, taking with it her last hope at happiness.

When she heard the front door slam shut, she stumbled over to the window, her legs nearly buckling under her, her hands propelling her along the smooth desktop.

A cold, clammy sweat settled on her skin as she watched him drive off into the pale misty morning.

One minute she'd had everything and now? She had nothing. Giovanni would forgive anything but not loving him enough, not returning the passion he felt for her, not trusting him.

She slumped down into the chair beside the window, images of Giovanni's confrontation with Alberto flashing into her mind, out of sequence, without meaning. Giovanni had been in complete control. By bringing in the police, he'd ensured justice was done. She hadn't given him enough credit.

She hadn't trusted him enough.

Two things were certain. He was right. And he wouldn't be coming back for her.

She pushed herself up and looked out at the slowly awakening world, shaking her head. She couldn't live without him. She couldn't see a future without him. He must come back.

And perhaps he would. He was hasty, perhaps he would return shortly with flowers, with anything, with just himself. She pressed her face to the window—her vision blurred with tears. There was no sign of him.

Slowly her focus withdrew from outside and she saw herself in the light of the desk lamp—reflected back to her in the window—ghost-like, white-faced, her hair crazily wild, tumbling around her face. Shocked to see this outward vision of herself when so much of her reality was centered on her emotional turmoil, she recoiled.

She turned sharply away. Her gaze swept the room. Unimportant papers were strewn around the room. The shredder filled with millions of pieces of important papers. Her laptop destroyed.

Pointless, she thought. Alberto must have known she'd have copies, that she would have stored such important information in a number of different places that were secure and impossible to find. And yet he'd come here to destroy the evidence.

She lay down on the bed and curled up into a ball, too stunned for tears, too wired for sleep.

He hadn't come here to destroy the evidence, she realized numbly; he'd come here to destroy Giovanni through her. And he'd succeeded.

Where was Giovanni now? The pain of wanting him forced her off the bed again. He'd come. He had to. She'd tidy the room, that's what she'd do. And shower. And get ready, because he would be back. He had to come back.

BUT THE DAY passed into night, and night passed into day again and the next morning saw Rose shivering, dry mouthed and red-eyed beside the open window once more. Her head resting against the folded-back shutter, she stared out into the slowly lightening sky. The long night had been a confusion of strange, sporadic dreams and cruel awakenings.

Stiffened by the night air, her sleep had merged almost seamlessly with her consciousness until there had seemed no end and no beginning, only the pain of wanting and waiting.

It was as if her body had ceased to exist, so divorced was she from physical feeling. She knew she should feel pain from the places Alberto had hit her, but there had been nothing. Simply a sickening need that she realized would never now be filled.

But a small part of her kept on hoping; made her stay by the window, even as the light slowly grew into the gentle, long drawn out dawn of summer. She recognized the beauty of the early light flickering through the leaves of the stately plane trees that lined the street but felt nothing of it. She heard the brief chorus of birds that took refuge in that old and leafy part of Milan, but felt no joy.

All she could think of was the look on Giovanni's face when he'd realized that she hadn't trusted him with the truth.

Up until then, he'd believed she'd told him everything; he'd believed that she'd trusted him; he'd believed that he'd been able to show her that he could be trusted.

But she hadn't.

She closed her eyes and pressed her forehead against the cool windowpane. Why not? Because she was too afraid. Afraid that her world would fall apart if she gave even one small iota of herself to another person. But her world had fallen apart anyway, because of her fear. And she'd been too stupid, too blind to understand.

But Giovanni had understood and he'd been patient. He was right. He'd made all the changes, he'd done everything to make it work. And she'd done nothing. It had been her fear— her selfish needs—that had come first.

She looked outside at the strange mixture of people walking along the ancient road that led to the heart of the city and wished she were one of them: one of the street's wealthy inhabitants, jumping into a car, or one of the tourists, soaking up the atmosphere, in awe of the beauty that surrounded them.

But she wasn't one of them. She leaned back. There was nowhere to run any more. Because she realized she'd been running from herself.

A car horn blared and she looked up suddenly. A tourist leaped to safety and the car continued on its way.

It was as if she'd awoken from a trance. She sat up and looked at the clock. Six a.m. She'd start ringing around. Someone must know where he was.

THE HOURS PASSED. In between intermittent flurries of telephone activity Rose found herself back at her window watching and waiting.

It was only when the street lamps flicked on that she

finally allowed herself to face the truth. She'd tried everyone but Giovanni was untraceable, unable to be contacted. And now it was evening once more.

A warm, damp mist had descended into the wide valley, unmoving and smothering. There was a sense of expectancy in the still air, of an end drawing near. And, now that she was physically stronger, she realized that Giovanni had made himself quite clear. He was simply not coming back while she was still here. It was up to her to bring closure. She owed him that much.

But there was one last thing she wanted to do. She'd have to wait one more night.

THE TAXI DRIVER tossed her bags into the back of the taxi.

"You may have to wait, signora, until it opens. It will cost if you want me to wait."

"That's fine. I don't have to be at the airport until late morning."

He drove like a lunatic through the streets that were relatively quiet as darkness seeped away to the west, the rising sun igniting the top of the high towers with fire.

SHE SAT on the bench in the small piazza and waited and watched: watched as her taxi driver ordered a coffee and chatted with a street vendor; watched as joggers, immaculately attired even at that hour, ran through the streets and watched the pigeons whirl in the damp mist as the sun slowly rose in the sky, casting its rays through the high towers down to street level.

As the church bells chimed the hour an officious looking, perfectly coiffured woman opened up the church. Rose took a deep breath to calm her nerves. It was always hard saying goodbye. And it was here that she felt closest to him, now that he'd left her. The memory of their connection, of that moment when he'd asked her to marry him, was all she had of him now.

Rose's shoes clicked lightly on the floor of the Santa Maria presso San Satiro. The elaborate decoration on the walls—gold and black—soared all around her as she walked slowly towards the apse. There, she marveled once more at the artistry in the frescoes. Looking up, she could see the distant pink flush of sunrise coming through the high window.

She closed her eyes. If there was still any magic, let it come now, let it work for her.

She opened her eyes but nothing had changed. Early tourists were beginning to enter, wide-eyed, cameras clicking, along with genuine worshipers who silently slipped into the pews and bowed their heads.

She realized, then, that the magic hadn't come from the church, but from themselves. It had simply felt so powerful that she couldn't believe it had come from within.

She shivered. Just as she had all those years ago with Giovanni. But then, he'd put his arm around her and held her close, transferring his body heat to hers and making the miracle of love happen. Before they'd left he'd insisted that they light a candle. She hadn't understood it then. But she did now.

She walked over to the altar and dropped some coins into a box and picked up a candle. By the time it had sputtered and died, she would be out of the city.

"Where is she?"

"Signore, I—"

"Simon, where the hell is Rose?"

"She's not here, signore."

"What the hell do you mean? She was sick, she was recuperating. It's only three nights I've been away. How could she leave with injuries like hers?

She refused to see anyone, signore. Even the doctor. She insisted she was well."

"You should have made her see someone. Broken the door down if necessary. Anything. What the hell do I pay you for?"

Giovanni paced the floor, stabbing his cell phone for messages, while he continued to berate his assistant, who knew better than to respond.

"When did she leave?" He continued to pace, looking into her closet, checking what had been taken.

"Early, signore. No-one was around."

"I told you specifically that someone should stay on the premises."

"They did, signore, but they also need to sleep. She must have left before dawn."

Suddenly Giovanni stopped pacing and sat heavily in the chair, rested his arms on his legs and looked down at the floor.

"She's gone."

"Yes, signore, she has."

"You should have told me that she wasn't letting anyone see her. You should have contacted me and I'd have come."

"We tried, signore. *She* tried, many times. But we were unable to find you."

Damn Allegra. She'd always been too literal, too gullible. She'd obviously blamed Rose for what had happened to her.

"So you have no idea where she is?"

"No."

"Cuzzo!" He threw the phone to the ground; it skidded across the floor. "Cazzarola!" He turned to Simon. "Find her."

The quietness of his last words had Simon moving faster than he'd ever done before.

AN HOUR later he'd traced the cab that had picked her up and made sure it wasn't going anywhere else. Santa Maria presso San Satiro. Of course. He slammed the front door closed and started walking. He needed to walk. He couldn't sit in rush-hour traffic doing nothing. Besides, it would be quicker.

Collar up against the damp, hands thrust into his pockets, he walked quickly through the busy streets, full of angry self-recrimination. Why had he rushed off like that? He'd known what she was trying to tell him but he'd been so angry with her. And so angry with himself. It had been *his* brother who had done this to her. *His* family. And he hadn't been able to make everything right.

He'd been punishing her for his deep feelings of guilt. He'd driven all day and lain awake all night. Three nights. Three nights wasted when he could have been with Rose.

Stupid, he told himself, as he crossed a busy street, narrowly dodging the cars that raced by.

Anger still pulsed in his veins at the fact that she hadn't told him everything, hadn't trusted him after all they'd been through. But, as she'd said, trust had to be earned.

A blare of car horns made him stop. In front of him was the church. It was his last chance.

A SHADOW PASSED over the light of the flame that filtered through Rose's close eyelids.

She rose shakily to her feet.

"Giovanni? What…?"

"What am I doing here? Looking for you." He paced

around her. She could feel his anger emanating in waves from him.

"Why?"

"Unfinished business."

"Business? Is that what this is about? Work? Allegra must have found all my documents by now."

"I don't want your documents."

"What then? Tell me now and tell me quickly." She could feel hope surge within. She needed to know quickly.

"To give you a chance…"

He trailed off, as if, for once, he were at a loss for words.

"A chance to apologize? You want me to apologize? I'm sorry. I'm so sorry. You were right." She waited, trembling. What would he do now? Turn around and leave?

"I don't want your apologies."

"What do you want then? For Christ's sake tell me what you're here for." Her head throbbed from her wounds and she sat back down back on the hard pew.

"I want you."

Hope sprang into her heart.

"Because I haven't finished with you yet."

Only to be immediately extinguished. "I'm not your plaything. Stop messing with me, Giovanni. I thought this was all over."

"It's not over. Not for me. How can it be when I feel you here," he grabbed her hand and pressed it against his heart.

Shocked and speechless she stood with her hand still pressed against his heart.

"And you can't deal with that can you? My passion."

She shook her head. "You've got it wrong. I can't live without it. I'm tired of living in fear of life, in fear of passion. Without it? I have nothing. Only a half life; no life. I need you Giovanni, like I need the air to breathe. I need you to touch and hold me. Otherwise there is nothing."

She waited for his response. There was none. Seconds past and he looked at her, his face a mask in the dim light of the church.

"You don't like making life easy for me do you, *cara?*"

She shook her head and pressed her forehead against his chest. She couldn't stop shivering.

"I'm cold, Giovanni. I'm so cold."

He drew her to him, oblivious to the people milling around, and held her tight against his chest. She could hear his heart beating against her face.

He pressed his cheek to the top of her head.

"I'll warm you."

"I think it will take a lifetime to thaw me out."

He touched her cheek, covered with a dressing and kissed the top of her head where stitches were visible in her hair.

"Lucky for you, I have a lifetime."

"But how can you forgive me?"

"I needed to earn your trust, Rose. Give me time. Let me show you. Whatever you can give me, I will hold and cherish. You will not be the less for having given it to me. It will not weaken you; it will strengthen you. I swear."

She held him tight, trying to stop the shaking, feeling his warmth and love force the fear from her soul. Trusting in Giovanni would be like trusting in herself—they were as one.

The magic of the church was still there. But she knew, now, that it wasn't external; it came from their hearts. And it was a magic that would stay with them—always.

Four months later...

Rose paused for a moment as she caught sight of Giovanni. He looked a solitary figure, surrounded by the blaze of reds, coppers and ochres of autumn leaves, as he gazed out across the misty lake to Lugano. She walked up behind him and slipped her hands around his waist and rested her cheek against his back.

"You're deep in thought."

He pressed his hands over hers. "It's time for us to leave, Rose. We can't stay here forever."

"I know." She brushed her face against the soft cotton of his shirt, relaxing as the heat of his body warmed her. "Part of me doesn't want to, it's so peaceful here." She paused as she thought again how to express her meaning. She'd never hide her thoughts from Giovanni again. "*I'm* so peaceful here."

He turned in her arms and smiled down at her. "Peaceful? That's not something you've ever associated with me before."

"I'm peaceful *because* of your passion, not despite it. I'm ready to move on now. So long as you're with me."

He slid his hands down her arms and gripped her hands tightly. "I'll always be with you."

"I'm counting on it." She felt the crisp scalloped edge of notepaper in his hands and looked down—gold edged, expensive stationery. "A letter? From your mother?"

"And how did you know that?"

"The paper. It's the sort your mother uses. Besides, no-one else I know sends letters any more."

"Yes, it's from Mama. With Alberto locked up in Switzerland, she wants to remain in Paris where she can visit him regularly, but avoid the scandal that surrounds her here, in Italy. I doubt she'll ever return to Milan."

Rose exhaled a long slow breath of relief and tried to be generous. "Sounds like she's found a life for herself in Paris, a better one."

"She's sorry, you know, for how she treated you."

"Yes, she told me. We're fine now, but…"

He lifted her chin. "It's hard to forget, no?"

She nodded.

"That's why I want to begin a new life, Rose, with you, somewhere else."

Rose stepped away in astonishment, searching his face for answers. She'd always imagined they'd return to the Milan mansion. Her heart thumped heavily with excitement. "Really? But what about the house?"

"I've given it to my cousins. I know you never liked the place and now," his smile dropped, "now, I want a fresh start."

Relief flooded her. "Sounds good to me."

"Where shall we go?"

"What about the business?"

"That's no problem. I'll restructure, move the head office

to wherever we want to be. New Zealand? Europe, the States?"

"Well, we're back in New Zealand next month for a visit."

"Ah, yes, your scholarships." He grinned. "They seemed very pleased when I let them know the identity of their mysterious benefactor."

She shook her head. "You are incorrigible, Signore Visconti. Still, it'll be good to meet them. And, then afterwards, we can see where we want to be."

"Perhaps an apartment in Milan until we decide? It will be easier than working from Lugano. Something small and simple." He cast her a wicked glance. "Perhaps just one large bedroom."

She pressed her face against him, trying to contain the bubble of excitement. "It would have to be a large apartment."

"Yes, I realize you'd like visitors. We can have an adjoining apartment for them, if you wish."

"No. I was thinking of something bigger, at least two bedrooms."

He frowned. "If you sleep in a separate bedroom, I will simply follow you. There is a limit to how much a possessive lover can reform."

She laughed. "You might *want* to be in a separate bedroom at some point."

"Never." His lips captured hers in a swift kiss. He frowned again. "What is all this about? You're different today." His eyes roamed her face and she tried to look away so she didn't reveal what was dominating her thoughts. She started to laugh as he moved his head in line with hers. "Your cheeks are flushed," he managed to capture her face in his hands, "your eyes are bright and yet you should be tired after last night."

"And this morning. Don't forget this morning."

He narrowed his eyes. "How could I?" He paused and looked her long and hard in the eyes, as his hands swept around her body and over her breasts before resting on her hips, his thumbs stroking her stomach. Then he stood back as if struck.

"You're pregnant."

"How did you know?" Her obvious irritation had the opposite effect on Giovanni and his grin broadened as his hands sought her body even as she fought him off, annoyed that he'd pre-empted her news.

"Pregnant. *Dio!* That is wonderful news! *Fantastico! Magnifico!*" He kissed her so gently, that her irritation evaporated and tears pricked her eyelids. He pulled away with sudden decision. "Come, we need to go."

She fell into step beside him, his arms still tightly around her. "Back to Milan?"

"Are you mad?" He looked at her with intensity. "No, *cara*, back to bed."

She laughed. "But you said we need to return."

"One more day…" He leaned down and brushed his lips against hers.

"And then another…" She rested her head against his shoulder.

"And then another…" He kissed the top of her head. "And it will still not be enough."

~

THE END

AFTERWORD

Dear Reader,

I hope you enjoyed Giovanni and Rose's story. Reviews are always welcome—they help me, and they help prospective readers to decide if they'd enjoy the book.

The **Italian Romance** series continues with book 4, *An Accidental Christmas*, an excerpt of which follows.

If you enjoy reading about alpha heroes and the strong women they fall in love with, why not try my sheikh books which include the **Desert Kings** and **The Sheikhs of Havilah** series? Turn the page to find out more!

Find out more about all my books on my website —http://www.dianafraser.net/.

Happy reading!

Diana

An Accidental Christmas

Ursula has given up on Christmas and is doing her level best to avoid it—family, presents, traditions—the whole package. Trouble is, when she becomes lost in the snowy mountains of Italy, with a car that won't start, and nowhere to stay, she finds she's landed in the midst of a traditional Christmas with no place to hide.

Widower Demetrio is devoted to his family, his land and tradition. And then he falls for Ursula—a beautiful woman from a very different world to his—and knows he has to get her to fall in love, not just with him, but his life. So he tempts her... one tradition in return for one more day together.

But can Demetrio's traditions and love do the impossible? Can they make Ursula stop running from her emotions, and instead, embrace them?

Excerpt

They walked carefully toward the frozen waterfall--its long, sleek plumes of water hard and unreal. At that moment, the sun rose over the hillside casting its bright light onto the ruffled sheets of ice. Ursula had never seen anything as beautiful--not in her native Sweden, nor in any of the cosmopolitan cities in which she spent most of her life. "It's stunning."

She turned to him and met his gaze. "Stunning," he repeated. But he wasn't looking at the frozen waterfall, only her. She suddenly felt self-conscious and pulled the soft gray hat that Marianna had lent her, lower over her blonde hair. She smiled uncertainly. "Come, on. I can see you're still not persuaded about the magic."

He walked carefully along the ledge which ran between the sheet of ice and the rock face. Ursula felt a flutter of nerves but was urged on by the warm, confident grip of his hand. She stepped behind the curtain of ice, and was robbed of breath.

The sheet of ice was aqua blue from behind. She reached out to touch it, but his grip on her other hand tightened, warning her not to move. She withdrew her outstretched hand. She didn't need to touch it to appreciate it. "You're right. It is magic." At that moment, a stray beam of sunlight penetrated the ice and illuminated the mossy green of the wall behind, splitting the light into a rainbow of colors.

Inexplicably Ursula felt tears prick her eyes. What was going on? She never cried. She turned away so he couldn't see her expression because she was afraid her defenses were blown. She sucked in the icy cold air, its frigid temperature searing her lungs and drying the tears. She turned and smiled. "Magic," she repeated.

With his eyes never leaving hers, he lifted her chin with his finger and kissed her, light as a feather, on her mouth. His finger swept her jaw before he stepped away. "I'm sorry. You looked irresistible with the word 'magic' still lingering on your lips."

Buy Now!

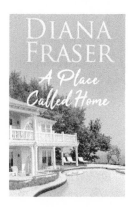

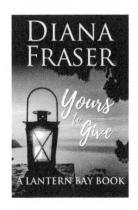

Desert Kings

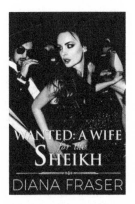

Claimed by the Sheikh

Wanted: A Baby by the Sheikh

The Sheikhs of Havilah

The Sheikh's Secret Baby

Bought by the Sheikh

The Sheikh's Forbidden Lover

Surrender to the Sheikh

Secrets of the Sheikhs

Italian Romance